Death

CARIDAD PIÑEIRO

MILLS & BOON®

Pure reading pleasure™

First published in Great Britain 2008
by Harlequin Mills & Boon Limited,
Eton House, 18-24 Paradise Road, Richmond, Surrey TW9 1SR

© Caridad Piñeiro Scordato 2006

ISBN: 978 0 263 86006 1

46-1108

Harlequin Mills & Boon policy is to use papers that are
natural, renewable and recyclable products and made from
wood grown in sustainable forests. The logging and
manufacturing processes conform to the legal environmental
regulations of the country of origin.

Printed and bound in Spain
by Litografia Rosés S.A., Barcelona

ABOUT THE AUTHOR

Caridad Piñeiro was born in Havana, Cuba, and settled in the New York metropolitan area. She attended Villanova University on a presidential scholarship and graduated magna cum laude. Caridad earned her Juris Doctor from St John's University and became the first female and Latino partner of Abelman, Frayne & Schwab.

Caridad is a multi-published author whose love of the written word developed when her fifth-grade teacher assigned a project – to write a book that would be placed in a class lending library. She has been hooked on writing ever since. Articles featuring Caridad's works have been published in various magazines and newspapers.

When not writing, Caridad is a mum, wife and lawyer. Caridad also teaches workshops on various topics related to writing and heads a writing group at a local bookstore. For more information on Caridad's books, contests and appearances, or to contact Caridad, please visit www.caridad.com.

To my editor, Stacy Boyd,
who believed in this concept from the
beginning and whose keen editorial sense
has helped me grow as a writer.
Stacy – you are the best!

Chapter 1

Like the phantom pain of a lost limb, the memory of Ryder's bite lingered, reminding her of what he'd done. Reminding her that she'd begged for his violence.

There was no scar at her neck. No fresh wound, raw and bleeding. Instead, the pain was deep inside, as alive in her heart as the day two years ago when her lover had first revealed his vampire nature.

Before Ryder, she hadn't allowed herself to feel anything for anyone, not since her father's death. That she had lowered her defenses and made love with him only to find out he was a vampire had awoken the rage and anger she had thought under control. Dealing with it had been difficult.

Now, it was almost as painful to acknowledge where their two-year love affair had led them—

to the wreckage of her carefully recon-
structed life.

Diana grabbed her shot of Cuervo and downed
it in one gulp. Then she immediately signaled the
bartender for another. But she only stared at the
drink in front of her, fingers splayed on the
scarred black surface of the bar.

The Blood Bank was a favorite haunt of those
in Manhattan's vampire subculture and a great
place if one wanted to offer themself up as a treat.
But after the day she'd had she only wanted to lick
her wounds and hopefully not add any fresh ones.

She didn't want anyone to put the bite on her.
Not even Ryder. Not again. Okay, *maybe* not
again, she confessed when the heated recollection
of their passion replaced the warmth of the tequila.

A reaction that reminded her all too vividly of
why she was here, bleeding on the inside and just
barely in control on the surface. A combination
sure to bring trouble.

By anyone else's standards, it had been an
ordinary day. Diana had met her best friend
outside a favorite Italian restaurant, a place Diana
hadn't been to in months. When, she'd wondered,

had she stopped going to her normal haunts and started going almost exclusively to Ryder's?

She'd dismissed the thought upon seeing Sylvia. There had been something different about her friend. She'd seemed positively radiant. Sylvia's coffee-brown eyes had glittered with joy and her smooth olive skin bore a vibrant blush. Eventually, Diana noticed the swell of belly. Her friend not only confirmed the happy news, but asked Diana to be godmother to the baby.

Diana had been happy for Sylvia. At least, that's what she'd told herself initially.

Until Sylvia glanced down at her belly and rubbed her hand lovingly over it. That motherly gesture drove an arrow of pain deep into the middle of Diana's heart.

Her doubts about Ryder, about their relationship, overwhelmed her. Doubts, that if she was honest, she'd been having for months, since her brother had announced the coming birth of his own child. Diana would never know the sensation of a baby growing and moving within her, of seeing herself fecund with child. At least, not if she stayed with Ryder. He was a vampire, undead. He couldn't bestow life.

"Are you going to put that drink out of its misery or let it sit there all night?"

Brought back to the present, Diana glared at Foley, the owner of the Blood Bank, as he perched on the bar stool next to her. As always, he was lethally elegant in a fitted black suit that punched up the paleness of his skin and hair and elongated the already sparse lines of his body. With a shrug meant to dissuade his attention, she replied, "I didn't know an inanimate object could feel misery."

The vampire's clear gray eyes darkened. With one finger, he traced her heart-and-dagger tattoo through the fabric of her suit. "They do when they could be in something as delicious as you."

Diana snared his hand and bent his thumb back at an awkward angle. "Don't go there."

Foley's grin didn't waver, although she knew that even with his vampire strength, she was likely causing some hurt. "Did you get that tattoo to prove how tough you are, Special Agent Reyes?"

She laughed harshly and increased the tension of her hold. "I got it to remind me of the pain."

"You enjoy it, don't you?" he asked. A sly look slid into his gaze, hinting that he rather liked the hurt she was currently inflicting on him. She let him go.

"I enjoy dishing it out."

In truth, the tattoo was a reminder not to act impulsively, a trait she had been accused of more than once. After a night of too much tequila, she'd gotten the tattoo to remind herself to guard against the pain she had suffered after losing her boyfriend. Only later did she realize that the knot of sorrow within her had been about the death of her father and all that she believed in. Justice. Honor. Happiness. Herself.

Sitting here, drowning her misery in tequila now, as much as she'd done at nineteen, warned her she was in danger of losing herself again as she had nearly a decade earlier when her dad had died.

"Bad day at the office, Special Agent Reyes?" Foley waved for a drink—a shot glass filled with liquid the color of ripe, succulent cherries. Freshly drawn blood.

"A nouveau Italian straight from Mulberry Street." He held the glass up in a toast.

Despite her earlier recollection about where one too many tequilas might lead her, she hoped a few more would create the right degree of numb. Help her forget about babies, husbands and houses filled with family—the kinds of things Ryder could never give her. She clicked her glass with Foley's and bolted back the Cuervo. The sting made her wince as the liquor burned its way down her throat. Slamming the glass onto the bar, she motioned for another.

"Extremely bad, I guess," Foley said, which only earned him a sidelong glance. He was sipping his drink slowly, savoring the grisly libation.

"What do you want?"

Foley leaned closer. So close that his chilled breath bathed the side of her face. With it came the metallic smell of blood. She almost gagged.

"Just to chat with a friend."

She gave him a forceful nudge in the ribs to remind him he had invaded her space. "You and I aren't—"

"Pals? Chums? Aren't you and Ryder… friendly?"

Ignoring him, she laid her hands on the bar's rough surface. Beneath her palms she registered the bumps, dents and gouges worn into it by misuse, by the violence for which the Blood Bank was known in the undead world. Again the phantom pain came to her neck and she inched her hand upward.

Foley ran the icy pad of his finger over the spot of the long-healed and invisible injury in a caress that made her skin crawl. "He's bitten you, hasn't he? More than once. And not just to feed. Yum." He smacked his lips with pleasure.

She yanked away from his touch, angry with his intrusion into her private life. "So what? Taking a survey?"

"With each bite his control over you grows. Your need for him intensifies until…"

You beg him to take you. To make you like him.

Which scared the shit out of her.

She prided herself on having learned control a long time ago. In the year following her father's death, she had lost her restraint and her identity in the ambience of places like the Blood Bank. It was only after waking one morning facedown in vomit, her younger brother passed out beside her, that she realized she was on the road to oblivion and taking her brother with her. She had mustered the strength to deal with her pain, to restore her sense of self and honor. It had taken her a long time to control her rebellion, to choose what she knew was right.

Lately she seemed to have less control over her emotions, over her choices, and worse, she didn't have a clue as to whether her relationship with Ryder was right or wrong. Which only partially explained why she found herself here, in a bar catering to the undead. Sharing a drink with a vampire who would drain her, given the right circumstances. Avoiding the lover who made her plead for a passion so intense....

That was the one thing she knew in her uncertain life. If Ryder was a drug, she was a Ryder junkie.

When she had first met him, Ryder had been living his life as humanly as possible. The attraction between them had been that of woman to man, man to woman. She hadn't known then just how hard it was for Ryder to control the beast within him. Or, worse, how much she would come to like the demon and what it made her feel.

The spot at her neck tingled again. When Ryder had been mostly human, she could tell herself their affair was right, but now that he was finally exploring his vampire powers, now that he was becoming less human she could no longer avoid the truth.

The change hadn't happened overnight. It was only in the past year or so, when they'd become more involved with Manhattan's other vampires, that Ryder had begun to change. She hadn't noticed at first, but recently it had become impossible to ignore. Ryder was darker and more powerful than she could have imagined. Worse yet, she liked his transformation. Too much.

And that was what troubled her the most— how much she wanted to share in his darkness, how much she craved the intense emotions only he could rouse. Was she losing herself to him?

Shaking her head to clear her thoughts, she half slipped off the high stool and tossed some money on the bar. Foley grabbed her arm, but she tugged free of his grasp. "Don't."

"Afraid?" His feral smile held a hint of fang.

But Foley's toothy smile didn't scare her. It only served to remind her of the vampire underworld that called to the darkness within her. A darkness she had thought she'd left behind after her father's death. One she didn't want to revisit.

"Screw you, Foley."

She walked away, chased by his laughter. Or maybe it was Foley calling, "Change your mind?" that pushed her onward.

She needed to be away from the Blood Bank and any other reminders of the surreal state of her life. She took a long walk before flagging a cab to go home.

Home. She needed to go home. Grab a pint of ice cream on the way and settle down to try to find some inner peace. Today had been just too normal. Lunch with a friend. The happiness and joy of Sylvia's coming child. The yearning for the contentment home and family could provide.

Even before Ryder, Diana hadn't thought much about that kind of life. Definitely not since becoming an FBI agent. Her career had taken up so much of her energy that she hadn't considered that at some point she might want…more.

But now she couldn't refute the possibilities and impossibilities. She had at one time thought she'd have a normal life. A husband and kids. Growing old. Dying. Everyday stuff.

She didn't want a life of the abnormal—one hidden beneath the surface of the city. She had existed like that once before and it had nearly consumed her.

Just as Ryder and his darkness would consume her if she didn't find a way to let go.

Monday was their night. His club was closed then, which meant they usually had the leisure of a long dinner, possibly a movie. Mortal things. Things that people who were dating regularly did.

Like making love. A maybe-not-so-mortal thing with them.

Was that why she had called tonight to tell him she didn't want to see him?

She'd been that blunt. Diana wasn't the kind of woman who made excuses.

And he wasn't the kind of man to…

But he wasn't a man anymore, Ryder reminded himself as he perused the streets from the balcony of his apartment. Across the East River, the large red Pepsi and Silvercup Studio signs glowed. The erratic string of lights from the bridge and Roosevelt Island tramway twinkled. In the water there were a few scattered boats, not many.

It was late, although in the city that never slept, the activity was incessant.

Where was Diana in all that activity? Holed up in her office working on a case? Asleep in her apartment? Or somewhere else?

The last possibility bothered him more than he liked to admit. He had never considered himself a jealous man. But then again, he had never met a woman as complex and independent and as deliciously dark as Diana.

Ryder grew hard and his fangs elongated as he recalled their last bout of sex. She'd moved beneath him, pleading for his possession. For his bite.

Her blood had been sweet, spicing his mouth as she'd cried out her completion. He had become nearly feral with feeding from her body as he'd driven into her. Her blood, providing him…so much life.

He growled and shook his head to chase away the demon, the animal that had almost not let up the other night. He had come close to draining her. Had nearly made her like him, because she called to him like nothing else in his undead life. Now, he couldn't just stand there, wondering.

He sprung over the ledge of his balcony like a gymnast vaulting over a horse and landed on the balcony of the floor below, where Melissa—the doctor whose family legacy was to care for his vampire health and serve as his keeper—now lived with her husband.

He caught but a glimpse of her, belly large with child. She stroked a hand across her extended abdomen with a beatific smile on her face. A moment later, her husband—Diana's younger brother—Sebastian walked into the room, a similar grin on his features as he laid his hand over hers.

Ryder couldn't linger. The scene was too painful a reminder of the life taken from him so long ago. Of the life he would be stealing from Diana if they continued their relationship.

Or if he sired her.

After biting her the other night, he had been forced to acknowledge just how badly he wanted her with him forever. After more than a century of avoiding humans and their emotions, he had allowed himself to care for her. She had restored him. Made him alive again. Losing her…

He knew pain. For close to one hundred and forty-three years, he had lived with the anguish of loved ones dying, of having everything familiar change. His response had been to shut himself off from other vampires, from humanity. From love.

But now, because of Diana, he was no longer alone. Would he be able to handle the pain of her death? Unsettled by those thoughts, he leaped down, floor by floor, to the street below. Once there, he hesitated, uncertain of where he would go. Unsure that it was wise to give in to the beast who longed for more than just seeing her.

For so long he had controlled his vampire nature and striven for a human life, the kind of life he had lost during the Civil War.

He didn't really understand how the sheltered existence he had so carefully built had become filled not only with Diana, but with an assortment of people and vampires who demanded he acknowledge what he was.

After despising his vampire nature for more than a century, he hadn't expected ever to enjoy the power and passion and strength that releasing the demon would bring. For so long, he had kept the beast at bay, afraid of what it could do. He had seen the aftermath of vampire violence against others, against himself.

A physician before a supposed act of kindness had turned him, he had devoted his life to healing, to saving others. He hated that the demon within was the total antithesis of what he had been—a good man.

But over the past two years, he had discovered that he could use his vampire powers for good— if he could control the violence that accompanied the demon. The violence it was becoming harder and harder to restrain around Diana. Was it because the beast didn't want to lose a mate after so much time alone?

Tonight the demon screamed for him to let it loose. Reluctantly he did. With a quick look to make sure no one was watching, he transformed. Long fangs erupted from his mouth and blood surged through his veins. All around him, colors and noises became more vibrant. Sounds sharper, almost painful to his heightened hearing. Smells, all those luscious smells, ripe around him. And beneath it all, the awareness of the humans close at hand, throbbing with life.

Speed beyond that of a mortal drove him. Where, he didn't quite know. He just reveled in the freedom of the night. The piercing glow of the moon and stars lit his way. The chill of the night

air flew against his heated skin. As he brushed
past one human on a side street, the scent filled
his nostrils. The thunder of heartbeat and blood
called to him. Sweet blood, pulsing.

Ryder badly wanted a taste. He imagined
sinking his fangs through fragile skin before his
mortal side rose up, reining in the vampire and
urging him to a nearby rooftop. Hurtling from
one edifice to the next, he reached an old and
narrow cobblestone alley in Tribeca. The Blood
Bank.

Hunger gnawed at his stomach.

Ryder stared at the entrance to the club. He
didn't normally frequent the place, not much
caring for Foley, the owner, or for the other
vampires who so blithely indulged their baser in-
stincts there, without a care. Without conscience.
Totally unlike the vampires he had befriended in
the past year. They tried to live nearly human lives.
They also refused to feed from humans and didn't
sire others like themselves. At least, they usually
didn't.

Ryder had learned from his new friends that
despite their best intentions, sometimes the beast
won out. Their experience had confirmed what

he'd already known—balancing his mortal and demon sides required dedicated effort.

So now here he was, the pit of his stomach clenching at the thought of fresh blood. Saliva pooled in his mouth like that of a hungry man sitting at a feast. Shaking his head, he took a deep breath to quell the demon's urges—and smelled her.

Diana.

She had either been nearby recently or was still close. Inhaling sharply, he picked up her scent and threw himself over the ledge of the building. He landed on his feet as quietly and gracefully as a panther on the prowl.

Her smell grew stronger at ground level. Ryder followed it to the door of the club, flashed some fang to get past the bouncer and hurried within, eager for even a glimpse.

She had made her feelings known, but one night away from her…was like an eternity.

In the stifling lifeless air of the club, Diana's smell strengthened and he followed it to the bar. She sat with Foley, letting the vampire lean toward her, touch her.

Ryder fisted his hands, barely controlling the desire to rip Foley's finger off.

With perverse satisfaction, he smiled as Diana did some damage of her own, but Foley, sick animal that he was, kind of liked it. *So do you,* his inner voice rebuked. *You like the violence she hides at her core.*

Anger barely subdued, he stepped into the shadows. The noise and music were too loud and uneven for him to make out their discussion. Interminably long minutes passed before Diana left.

Ryder hesitated, debating whether to follow Diana or to beat Foley into monster mash. First, because the vampire had touched Diana. Second, because Ryder had never liked Foley. He was everything Ryder hated and never wanted to be: a hedonistic animal, devoid of any mortal sensibilities.

And for some reason, Diana had ditched him for the undead cad.

Ryder's human side urged him to curb his resentment. After all, she had left the bar alone and rebuffed Foley's sole advance. But the demon… The demon damn well wanted some satisfaction.

Satisfaction that words wouldn't provide.

Chapter 2

She was finally home.

Elation swept through Ryder as he stood on her fire escape. He waited at her window needing to see her. All he could think about was her, about being with her again—in spite of the withdrawal and anger he sensed from her. Those emotions screamed for his acknowledgment. She was angry because he was visiting. Uninvited.

From her bedroom door, she headed straight for the window, as if aware he was there.

Slipping over the edge of the fire escape, he plummeted a few stories before grabbing the railing to break his fall. It jangled loudly as it bore the brunt of his weight. He quickly eased closer to the building and its shadows so he would be hidden. He soon heard the grate of the lock, the slight groan of recalcitrant metal as she opened the window. Then he smelled her. He breathed in deeply, trapping her essence within him. It was food for his senses, instantly bringing his body to painful life.

Not for the first time, he conceded that he liked certain abilities given to him by his vampirism. The ones that let him smell her and see her and, lately, reach into her mind to share his thoughts. She had allowed that new gift, although he knew she was uncomfortable with the invasion. She was, after all, a woman used to being in total control.

Was that why she was running from him?

He climbed onto the railing and, bunching the muscles of his legs, leaped up three stories to her window. He landed nearly silently and smiled to himself, pleased with how his skills were improving.

Now, he intended to make his presence known.

Ryder was here.

Damn him. It was bad enough he haunted her every thought and made her need him in ways she didn't want to need anyone. It was even worse that he refused to honor her one simple request for a night away from him. A night to try to forget what he made her feel so she could gain some peace of mind, if only for a moment.

You can never forget me, she heard inside her head.

Really? And could you forget me? she questioned angrily.

Never.

Maybe a little mental and physical anguish of his own would drive the point home: their relationship had taken a wrong turn. The reality she had confronted earlier—that she wanted a normal life—was impossible if she continued on this path. Ryder could never give her that kind of existence.

She faced the window and yanked off her suit jacket. Beneath the jacket, her holster securely cradled her Glock. She slipped it off, checked to make sure the safety was on and tucked the holster and gun into the drawer of her bedside table.

A gun would be no protection against Ryder. Especially when she hadn't loaded it with the special silver bullets she'd had made for when she went out on a vampire-related problem.

Do you really think you need to protect yourself against me?

No, but you might need to protect yourself, querido.

His uneasy chuckle carried through the open window of her bedroom.

Your amusement will stop soon enough.

Silence followed her threat.

Diana began to disrobe, a slow striptease as she slipped free each button of her serviceable white shirt, revealing the lacy white bra beneath. She toed off her ankle-high boots, and kicked aside her pants. *Do you like what you see?*

A strangled laugh was his answer, coupled with, *I haven't seen enough to make up my mind.*

She smiled. There was something…exciting about mentally seducing a vampire who was hidden in shadow.

She had experienced this kind of nasty excitement after her father's death. The rush of losing all restraint. The surrender to doing whatever you wanted, even though you knew it was wrong. Her reckless nature had embraced the uncivilized, the raw need that had never really surrendered to her control.

As for her earlier decision not to see Ryder… It fled in the wake of her rising desire.

Diana shrugged her shoulders and her blouse dropped to the floor. Reaching up, she undid the front clasp of her bra.

His rough groan caressed her psyche. And then a shadow shifted on the fire escape. Ryder's shadow.

Staring straight at him, she parted the bra and let it fall. She stood there, expectant. Her pulse racing.

Her earlier thoughts about needing something more normal—more controlled—reared up, telling her that she should ask him to leave. She had proved her point, reminding him that she had power, but her determination failed her.

I want you to touch me, she told him.

But he stayed on the fire escape, exerting a self-control she couldn't muster.

Closing her eyes to block out the sight of his silhouette, she cupped her breasts and ran her thumbs across her nipples. Her body grew damp and tense with rising need. With want of his hands and mouth and…his bite.

Dios, but she couldn't forget how the demon made her feel.

Ryder.

A thud forced her eyes open. He stood by the

window, dressed in black, breathing roughly, fists balled at his sides. His nearly black hair, long and tousled, hung to his shoulders. The goatee surrounding his mouth…

She imagined how that would feel on her skin and then had little time to wait as he stalked over, dropped to his knees and took one aching nipple into his mouth.

She moaned and dug her hands into the waves of his thick hair.

"I'll take it that you like that." Despite his chuckle, a hard edge marked his voice.

As conflicted as she might be about their future, it was impossible to deny that, at least right now, she wanted him, no matter what. No matter that by the wanting, she lost a piece of herself.

The inky locks of his hair were a shock of darkness against the pale creaminess of his skin and her own olive coloring. The contrast made her ache inside as her excitement escalated. Whenever he was near, her senses were on overload, with everything more clear and alive. More demanding.

"I want you." His brown-eyed gaze was so intense it made her insides quiver.

"As much as I want you—"

"You've been doubting the wisdom of this. I know. I felt it…. You didn't want me here to-night, did you?"

"No." But she raked her hands through his hair, the silk of the longer strands alive in her hands. He had let it grow since she had first met him.

"I know it scares you—the need. But don't you think I need you as badly? Or can't vampires need?" He once again tortured her by running the soft bristle of his beard across her nipples. But that wasn't her undoing. It was the confusion and pain that laced his words. Confusion much like she was feeling. Pain so deep her heart faltered from it.

"I care for you, only… Foley says that each bite—"

"I won't bite again," he said. *Not unless you ask me to.*

"I won't ask again. I can't lose myself like this. I can't stay with—"

"Don't push me away, darlin'. I know you're scared, but I am, too. In all my life, you're the only woman I've ever…"

Ryder didn't finish. Instead he buried his head against her midsection and wrapped his arms tight around her like a supplicant embracing his reason for being. Then he shocked her by kissing the scar along her ribs—a product of the drive-by shooting that had killed her father.

Diana closed her eyes against the sudden threat of tears and the constriction that closed her throat. She cradled his head and stroked his hair, trying to ease his pain. Trying to curb her own.

She might tell herself that she was afraid of what was happening with them. Of how he invaded her senses and her mind. She might even delude herself into believing that she could make love to him tonight or any other night and walk away whenever she wanted. But in her heart, she suspected that what she felt for him she would never feel for anyone else.

She wasn't sure she could live with that, but she couldn't deny him, either.

She made the next move. She parted the fine black linen to reveal his chest. Nothing marred the pale expanse of his skin. If anything, his muscles were more defined than when they'd first met. His body leaner, more…powerful. The energy seemed to pour off him, calling to her.

She laid her hand above his heart. It beat fast

and a little erratic. She wanted to believe its hurried rhythm came from her touch.

"I don't regret…us," she whispered. Funny, but it was the truth despite her doubts. He was her damnation and her salvation.

"Let's not talk about this now. The night is short and…I don't want to spend it…"

Burying her head against his chest, she wrapped her arms around him. Her embrace shook loose something inside of him.

He needed to make it impossible for her to deny that this was real, no matter how many doubts both of them now seemed to be having.

It was sweet torture, the feel of her breasts skimming his chest. Her warmth slowly worked its way into the cold of his body. The heat of her passion drove the chill from his skin.

She tugged him toward her bed. "This is what you want, isn't it?"

She wore her false bravado face. Funny how he could recognize it so easily. Funny how he wanted to drive the fear from her until she truly welcomed him into her bed. Invited him into her heart.

"Can you deny it's what you want, as well?" he said.

She couldn't lie to herself. She needed more of him. She always needed more even if she refused to give a name to that desire. Even as she wondered if it was a result of some vampire head game, much as Foley had suggested.

Ask me to touch you, he said.

Why?

His demanding reply came swiftly. *Because I need you to want me as much as I want you.*

"*Dios,* Ryder. I need you."

Slowly, way too slowly, he lowered his hand until it rested on top of the nest of curls between her legs. She pressed her hips up, urging him on. He breached the edge of her panties and unerringly found her center.

Beneath his fingers, Ryder experienced the pull of her. The scent of her arousal perfumed the air, so strong that the vampire within begged for a taste. He had lost the battle last time. He wouldn't allow it to happen tonight. If the animal came…she might hate him—or herself—for surrendering to the demon.

He dropped a trail of kisses along her body. She opened her legs, knowing his intent and welcoming it. He slipped between her legs, brought his mouth to her sensitive nub.

Her hips arched in acceptance.

Her wetness—slick against him—and the smell of her…the heat… He groaned and she held his head to her.

He lost the battle.

The change surged over him. It was almost too much. The smell of their sexual musk. Her racing pulse reverberating in his ears. Her nether lips, wet and flush with blood. The demon imagined feeding there, at her most private of places.

He gasped at the roiling passion making his loins ache and looked up at her with his vampire face. Fangs exposed. Eyes glowing. Skin flushed and warm.

Diana stared at him. His arms were braced at her sides, shaking. Shoulders heaving from the force of his breaths. His rough, harsh pants reminded her of a lion at a zoo, caged. The human in him was barely keeping the animal behind bars.

In her mind, suddenly, she saw herself as he did. Her breathing. Sharp little pants. His teeth, sinking into her swollen flesh. Blood, rich with life. Passion. Flowing through both of them. Charging them. Her strangled cry of pain followed by pleasure that would rob her of herself.

She nearly climaxed from the images. The vampire in Ryder wanted her to desire his bite, so he could do as he wished. So he could control her as Foley had warned.

She shook away those thoughts and with years of self-defense skills, reversed their positions. She drove down onto him before he could continue messing with her mind. With her heart. Riding him to slake the burn, to draw out the human, to make him Ryder again and not the beast.

As she locked her gaze with his and moved on him, the demon fled. Ryder's eyes became their intense dark brown once more, losing their demony glow. Only his fangs remained, as if he couldn't muster that last little bit of command.

"I won't bite again," Ryder promised.

Long minutes passed before she finally answered, "I know."

Without waiting for more assurance he flexed his hips and shifted upward, bringing her to the edge.

She followed his growl of release with her own cry of completion. After he cradled her in his arms. But earlier conflicts and fears rose up faster than the passion that had overwhelmed them.

When she had first met Ryder, she had sensed that he was a loner. A man who had suffered great loss and somehow endured. She understood such loss and the strength it took to overcome it. Like Ryder, she carried scars within her that hadn't healed.

Back then she'd thought that two injured people didn't bode well for a happy ending. And now, after tonight, she realized that continuing her life with Ryder…

"I'm not sure this is a good idea."

A tremor ripped through his body again. He snatched up the clothes strewn across the floor and dressed, his movements stiff. Irate.

"Ryder?" She heard fear and indecision in her own voice. And an indefinable something… caring, possibly love. She was too confused to know anymore.

He didn't answer. So she provided her own.

"I need some time."

A barely perceptible nod of his head acknowledged her request before he returned to her open window and fled into the night.

Chapter 3

The alarm beeped furiously. Diana half turned and shut off the noise. She had been awake for some time.

Was it her imagination or could she still smell him on her pillow?

It was barely 6:00 a.m., but she tossed aside the covers and rolled out of bed. The barest hint of red in the morning sky promised a clear day ahead. She would have time for a quick run before work.

Work, where things over the last two weeks had become routine. Normal. As they had been before Ryder.

A load of cases waited for her to profile. Two others were actively being investigated. Later that day, she had a much-anticipated lunch date with her FBI partner. Afterward, if she didn't get hung up too late with her active cases, she'd call Sylvia for a girl's night. It had been too long since they'd had one. Their last lunch together had reminded her just how much she missed seeing her friend.

Just as having dinner the other night with her brother Sebastian and his wife, Melissa, had demonstrated how removed she had become from her family. For years she and Sebastian had shared an apartment and they had always been close. After the death of their father, grief had united them even more strongly. But Sebastian's marriage to Melissa had complicated things, Melissa being Ryder's keeper and all.

Their recent carefree dinner, however, made it clear that whatever happened between Diana and Ryder would have little impact on her relationship with her brother. She'd had a wonderful time and had even gotten to feel the baby move.

Now, she shifted her hand downward, laid it over the flat, almost concave plane of her abdomen. Imagined a baby within. Alive. Its tiny heart fluttering beneath the palm of her hand. Growing and being born. Suckling at her breast.

In her mind's eye, the baby had Ryder's dark eyes and hair, but she forced that impossible thought away. Instead she remembered how her little niece or nephew had rolled beneath her palm. Sebastian had smiled at her reaction, looking happier than she had ever seen him.

Things were working out for him. He was all right.

Just as she was beginning to believe everything would be all right for her one day. The weeks away from Ryder had been hard, but with each day that passed, with each day of a human routine, she felt her control returning.

Each day brought more lightness to her spirit, something she hadn't felt in…forever.

She could imagine soon being back to a place where her life seemed in order. Where she could enjoy her friends and family. A good place.

Though more often then she cared to admit, Ryder slipped into her thoughts. Strange as it was, her life with him had in some ways made her believe anything was possible. But the unpredictability had kept her constantly on the edge. An edge that had grown difficult to walk.

Without him, however, a bit of emptiness existed that none of the routines of her day managed to fill. Routines that had, at one time, sustained her.

She told herself she just needed to relearn balance, the yin and yang of things. And that couldn't happen in only a couple of weeks. It would take time. Something Ryder had plenty of, while she… Her time was finite. Unless she gave in to the call of the demon.

She drove that thought viciously away.

She knew how hard life was for Ryder and his vampire friends. How they battled to contain the demon's desire for domination. How they suffered over and over again from the pain of who they had become, of losing those they loved.

Her father's death had taught Diana what it was to live with that kind of pain. She couldn't imagine living with it for eternity. She *needed* the everyday human world she had been struggling to reenter these past few weeks.

The cell phone on her nightstand vibrated. As she picked up the phone, the Caller ID indicated it was her friend, N.Y.P.D. Detective Peter Daly.

Whatever Peter had to say at this early hour couldn't be good.

"You're making a big mistake."

The sound of her shoes on the hard tile of the

police station hallway echoed as Peter escorted her to the interrogation room.

"Neighbors reported hearing a shot. Then we got Raul Rodriguez's 9-1-1 call. When we arrived, he was incoherent. The gun was on the bed where he had supposedly been asleep. And his wife—"

"Stop."

Raul's wife was Sylvia, who Diana had been thinking about calling only a short time earlier. It was impossible to believe her friend was dead.

"Diana. I know you're close to this—"

"She was one of my best friends. She asked me to be the godmother for their baby. Did you know that? Did you know she was pregnant?"

Peter had the grace to look chagrined. "Yes. I'm sorry."

"Sorry? Sorry!" Unable to control herself any longer, she faced the wall and pounded the rough cinder block with her fist.

Peter pulled her into a tight embrace as if to keep her from hurting herself. "I can't imagine how tough this is."

She held on to him, needing his stability because of all she was tempted to do. Sylvia's life—

her normal, happy, *human* life—was gone. Destroyed by violence. Violence like that within Diana, so strong she didn't know if she could hold it back. And if the killer turned out to be Raul...

Dios. She would give in to the darkness and kill the bastard herself.

"Di? You need to get a grip if you're going to talk to him."

With a deep shuddering breath, she pulled herself together. Stepping away from Peter, she wiped at her eyes. "Do we have any other leads?"

Frowning, Peter shook his head. "Everything we have points to the husband. Maybe he found out the baby wasn't—"

Diana silenced him with a pointed slash of her hand. "Don't go there. Sylvia didn't mess around," she said, then stalked down the hall to the interrogation room, Peter trailing behind her.

Raul sat at a Formica-topped table, jailbird-orange clothing hanging loosely on his hunched shoulders. His bloodstained pajamas had been taken as evidence. He was hollow-eyed and obviously still in shock. "Tell me what happened, Raul," Diana said.

"*No se.* We had dinner out. *Un poquito de vino,* but not much wine since Sylvia…" He stopped as tears spilled down his cheeks. He wiped at them with shaky hands and haltingly continued. "We went home. We were both really sleepy. As soon as my head hit the pillow, I was out." His hands tumbled in the air. "*No se que paso.* There was a sound. A loud sound. I started coming to, but everything was fuzzy…" He stopped once more, buried his head in his hands. The tears fell more furiously.

Diana laid a hand on his shoulder. "I know this is difficult, but you have to try to remember."

"I don't know what happened," he replied brokenly, and held out his hands as if pleading with her. "*De verdad que no se.* When I woke up, Sylvia was bleeding. I tried to wake her. When she didn't respond…I called 9-1-1. I held her. She was so still. Then I saw the gun."

"Did you touch the gun, Raul?"

He shook his head and wiped at his runny nose. "I don't remember touching it."

"Forensics will be able to confirm whether you did or not, Mr. Rodriguez. You may as well tell us now." Peter moved to the table.

Raul snarled at the detective, "I did not kill my wife. I don't know what happened, but I didn't do it. I *couldn't* do it. She was my life. *Mi vida*." He jabbed at a spot above his heart to emphasize the point.

The sincerity in his words convinced Diana. She touched Raul's clenched fist. "I believe you."

He slumped into his chair. "*Gracias*, Diana."

She glared at Peter. "I want to see all the reports. Anything you have."

"You're not assigned to this case. If the suspect hadn't asked for you—"

"I would have found out and—"

"You don't have jurisdiction here."

He was right. Taking a deep breath to control her anger and frustration, Diana nodded and followed Peter out of the room. Peter wouldn't refuse if she asked. So she did. "Ask me to help. I need to know what happened to my friend."

Peter gave her a long look. "Unofficially and…whatever I say goes on this one. I'm the lead."

"You're the boss, Detective Daly."

Peter let out a soft chuckle. "Right, Reyes. As if that will ever happen with any man in your life."

"May I see the evidence, Detective? Pretty please?"

Peter chuckled again and shook his head. "Cut the shit, Di. You don't do submissive very well."

No, she didn't, come to think of it. Maybe that was part of the reason her situation with Ryder troubled her so much. What she felt for him made her weak, made her surrender a piece of herself. She wasn't good about not being in charge.

"Okay, so I'm asking straight-up. Show me what you've got."

He motioned down the hallway. "CSU is processing most of it. But we can head to the M.E.'s to see the body—"

"Don't call Sylvia that."

Peter sighed and dragged a hand through his ragged sun-bleached hair. "I'm sorry. But you need to get perspective."

"I will deal with it. But if it were Samantha—"

"Low blow, Reyes," he said, his tone filled with anger at the idea of harm coming to his lover—who had sired Ryder more than a century earlier.

Ryder.

Like the intertwined strands on a web, everything in her life inevitably led back to him. Could she ever be truly free of him? Or would she be forever ensnared in that web, trapped by what she felt for him?

Had once felt for him, she reminded herself. As for those emotions and anything connected to them…she had to put them aside and focus on what was most important now—avenging her friend's death.

Diana let out an exasperated breath and laid a hand on Peter's sleeve. "I'm sorry. I will try to handle it better. Let's go see Sylvia. *Por favor.*"

She would do what needed to be done to find Sylvia's killer. And when she located him…

Living with vampires for two years had shown her just what she was capable of—fierce, swift action with no hesitation. Justice without the complicated rules of the human world.

She pitied Sylvia's killer when he, too, found that out.

Chapter 4

Just a few weeks ago, the swell of Sylvia's pregnancy had been a sign of hope for good things to come. Today, as Sylvia lay on the shiny metal of the medical examiner's table, it was a grotesque reminder of promises that would never be fulfilled.

Diana stood by patiently as the M.E. went over the details of the evidence. Bullet entry and exit wounds. Proximity of the muzzle—a close-contact kill with a large-caliber weapon, straight to the heart. Sylvia could never have survived the trauma. The delay in getting help had sealed the fate of the baby.

Gunpowder burns and stippling marked Sylvia's pajamas and skin. The bullet had gone straight through her and into the mattress below. CSU had recovered the bullet, but no casing. Ballistics was already attempting to link the bullet to the gun found and to any other crimes recently committed.

"Do you know if your friends owned a gun?" Peter asked as he picked up the .45 caliber revolver in an evidence bag.

"In law school Sylvia lobbied on behalf of the Assault Gun Ban. What do you think?"

With a quick nod, he held the bag out for the M.E. "Any prints?"

"Palm print as well as four fingers. We're running them now against the suspect." The M.E. reached into a tray holding more evidence and extracted a bag containing clothing. "Mr. Rodriguez's pajamas tested positive for blood in various locations, as well as high-velocity blood splatter along the right sleeve."

A possible inconsistency suddenly occurred to her. "Palm and fingerprints. Right or left hand?"

The M.E. flipped the bag containing the gun back and forth and examined the fingerprint powder residue. "Right."

"Raul's a lefty. Sylvia was always getting him those silly gadgets for lefties."

"That doesn't rule out that he used his right hand," the M.E. said.

Diana went over the M.E.'s earlier report on the entry and exit wounds. "He was lying on his side, facing her, when he did it."

The M.E. bobbed his head up and down. "That would explain the lack of defensive wounds. He could get the weapon in place and fire without her noticing."

"Or someone could put the gun in his hand, hold it in place and pull the trigger. Especially if Sylvia and Raul had been drugged. What about gunshot residue?"

"We haven't tested him for GSR yet. Before you arrived, he clammed up and asked for a lawyer," Peter said.

Years of experience had taught her that the innocent rarely felt the need for a lawyer, but then again, being married to an attorney might make Raul hesitant to provide assistance without legal advice. He had probably heard his share of horror stories from Sylvia about how things got twisted into something other than what they really were.

"The GSR test would confirm whether or not he was close to the gun when it was fired," Peter said.

"But not whether he was the one who actually

pulled the trigger," Diana reminded him. "The blood splatter pattern, however, might tell us."

With an annoyed sigh, likely at the prospect of doing additional work, the M.E. said, "Special Agent Reyes, you can't actually believe the husband didn't do it? The case is almost airtight."

"Airtight? If someone placed the gun in Raul's hand and pulled the trigger—"

"There would be an area on the sleeve that lacked splatter," Peter finished for her. "Have CSU check the entire right sleeve and make sure those toxicology reports are carefully reviewed for any unusual residues."

"Of course, Detective Daly," the M.E. answered. The glance he shot Diana was anything but friendly. As if to retaliate for the extra assignment the M.E. picked up the scalpel and let it linger above Sylvia's body. The light caught the sharp edge and a chill transferred itself to Diana's skin.

She had seen hundreds of autopsies before, but this one…

"I need to get back to the office." She bolted from the room, Peter hot on her heels.

"You okay?" he asked as she leaned against the wall outside the autopsy room.

Swallowing to keep down the bile, she could only nod. "Will you call me later? Let me know what's up and if toxicology finds something?"

"Will do."

As she started to walk away, he said, "Diana?"

"What?"

"Will you be all right?"

With a shake of her head, she said, "I wish I knew."

She couldn't face going home. Couldn't deal with sitting there alone, thinking about all that had happened. How what had started out as a normal day had spun into…darkness. As black and numb as that which had claimed her nearly a decade earlier.

Rushing out of her office, she started walking, headed nowhere in particular. Each step took her farther away from where she began, but no closer to where she needed to be. She wanted to be with other people, somewhere she could let go of the pain that had staked a claim on her this morning.

She could have gone to her brother, only she didn't want to drag him down with her misery. As for her partner, David had tried to help her upon her return to the office, but had failed miserably. Her wound had been too fresh for her to accept sympathy.

Her reaction to today's events was familiar, she realized. After her father's death, she had driven away those closest to her. Her *mami,* her then boyfriend and lover Alejandro, even Sebastian, at first.

A stitch in her side made her stop. She suddenly realized she had been running, attempting to escape her emotions.

Only there was no escape.

As she paused until her breath became regular, hands on her hips, she glanced down the street and realized she was only a block or two from Ryder's nightclub.

Had she been running to him or to the darkness she would find there?

With a deep inhalation, she told herself there was only one way to find out.

The Lair was the same as always. Charcoal-gray walls, structured to look like rock, absorbed most of the light, leaving the club with the feel of a subterranean chamber. Overhead, by the length of the stainless steel bar, hundreds of fake bats hung from the catwalks and ceiling. The only difference tonight was that the club was less crowded. It was early. So early that not even the band was on stage yet. Instead, music was piped in from a sound system.

Fine by her. Although she didn't want to be alone, Diana wasn't in the mood for masses of people milling around.

She couldn't feel Ryder, but then again, she couldn't feel anything but pain and anger. Loss. And worse than any of them combined, guilt— for not protecting her friend, for being absent from Sylvia's life so often lately.

She had been too busy with work—and with Ryder. Years earlier, she had experienced something similar. She had been too busy with college and with her boyfriend, too involved with the needs of her own life to have time for her father…

Until he was gone.

Grief squeezed her chest, making it difficult to breathe. She forced herself to move forward, but not toward the steps leading to Ryder's office. Not yet, anyway. Instead, she plunked herself down on a bar stool. Raising her hand, she motioned to the bartender she recognized from previous nights at The Lair.

The attractive blond laid out a coaster with the club's stylized bat-and-blood logo.

"A shot of Cuervo." Diana waved her hand toward the back of the club. "Is Ryder here?"

The girl shot a look up at Ryder's office window. "I don't think so."

So he *was* gone, Diana thought. She had suspected as much with the connection she *hadn't* felt from the moment she had stepped into the club. Maybe it was for the best. Maybe if he had been here tonight, she would have made a mistake she would so totally regret in the morning.

She rubbed at the tattoo on her shoulder, letting it remind her about not only protecting her heart, but avoiding rash actions. Seeing Ryder tonight likely being bad on both counts.

Diana slugged back the shot and then asked for another, which the bartender immediately supplied, although concern clouded her All-American features.

"Worried that I can't handle it?" Diana asked, both interested and amused by the young vampire's obvious anxiety.

The girl motioned to the tequila with a mani-cured nail done in pink. Nothing Goth about this vamp, Diana thought. "Last time I had one too many of those, I ended up undead."

Diana choked on her drink. "I'm sorry."

"Yeah, me, too. But I guess you go on, don't you?" She gave a careless shrug that couldn't quite hide the sorrow in her inquisitive blue eyes.

Diana only nodded her agreement. Was that why Ryder wasn't here? Was he going on, moving on? She peered around again, trying to open herself up to sense him.

"I don't think he'll be back for a while."

Diana experienced a rush of heat to her cheeks. "Am I that obvious?"

The vampire leaned her elbows on the bar and grasped the bar towel between both hands. "People tell me I'm intuitive. I guess that's why I get such good tips."

As Diana caught a glimpse of the cleavage the young vampire's current position exposed and shot her gaze up to the coed's too earnest and classically pretty features, she suspected there were other reasons, as well, but couldn't be cruel.

"You are that," she offered.

"So what about you and the boss man?" the vampire asked.

What *about* her and Ryder? "I'm not…like you." She looked down at her glass, a bit uncomfortable about reminding the unfortunate coed of her undeadness.

"Yeah. You're older," the bartender said, so matter-of-factly that Diana jerked her gaze up in surprise, only to find the girl smiling. A broad, fooled-you smile that was friendly and blasted away her earlier discomfort.

"You're right. I'm older and my clock—big tick tock. Settling-down time, *sabes?*"

"You don't seem like the home-and-hearth type."

Diana hesitated, thinking about the kind of life most people considered routine, about the kind of life she had finally acknowledged she might want. Except that lately an ordinary life seemed impossible.

Look at what had happened to her friend Sylvia. To *her* normal life. Look at what had happened in Diana's past.

The girl placed her hand on Diana's arm. "I never thought of myself as a soccer mom, either. I guess I should be glad I can avoid babies and wrinkles—"

"And sunburn," Diana tacked on, slightly renewed by the young vamp's honesty.

A wistful look came to the vampire's features. "I always did burn, but damn did I look good in a bikini."

Diana patted her cold hand. "It'll work out. I'm sure you've got friends here. Ones who will help you."

Some of the sadness faded from the girl's face as she nodded toward Ryder's office. "So do you."

A reluctant sense of rightness came to Diana as she realized the young vampire was right. For so long her mantra had been one of sticking to herself and limiting the circle of people around her. But now, she had an ever-expanding cadre of the living—and the undead—whom she could count as friends.

The sadness of her recent loss was slightly tempered as she met the bartender's gaze. "Maybe I do."

Chapter 5

Immobile as a gargoyle, Ryder balanced high on the edge of the building across from the church, watching over Diana in the crowd below. He had been lucky. The funeral was in the early morning and the day overcast enough to allow him the freedom of attending.

Diana hadn't called to tell him about her friend. She hadn't left a message at the bar, either, although the bartender had made a point of relaying that Diana had been by and appeared to miss him. Funny how Diana could spill her guts to a stranger, but be unable to convey anything to him about her emotions.

Not that she needed to tell him what she felt this morning, he thought. Grief etched lines on her face as she gripped the top of the gray casket and helped the other pallbearers wheel their burden to the uppermost step of the church.

Diana's steps were slow and measured, keeping pace with those in front of her. Each of the pallbearers peeled away until only Diana and a man stood at the back of the hearse. The husband, he suspected. They both stroked their hands over the surface of the casket one last time, and then the man embraced Diana and cried. His heartbroken sobs carried all the way to where Ryder perched. Diana tried to comfort the man, but her actions were stilted. Awkward. The lines of her body tense.

Luckily, someone from the family came to her aid and gently led Sylvia's husband to a limo. Others quickly followed, but Diana hung back, her eyes on the hearse.

Death sucked.

And being undead didn't make it any easier.

He had imagined too often lately how it would be after Diana died. He'd pictured the interminable days until they were reunited in the afterlife. The pain that came with such thoughts made him yearn to turn her, to keep her with him always. It was a desire he struggled with every day. And the struggle had kept him away from her.

Diana stood on the steps alone, clad in black, scoping out the church grounds.

Across the street someone with a camera busily snapped pictures. A few yards away at either end of the church, uniformed officers took down license plate numbers. Ryder had watched enough detective shows to realize they thought whoever had murdered Diana's friend might be in the crowd.

Ryder recognized one detective as Diana's friend, Peter Daly. He was clearly the leader of the investigation. Surprising. Especially since the murdered woman had been one of Diana's best friends. Ryder hadn't thought Diana would settle for anything less than being in command.

He didn't mind that she liked to take charge. He understood where the need came from. Her sense of control kept her balanced. That she could give up that control on such an important case was a new facet to his ex-lover.

He shifted his position on the ledge, inching closer in the hope of hearing their discussion. Of connecting with her telepathically as he'd done before, only…

Something blocked him. Whether it was intentional or not, he didn't know. He suspected the latter since he and Diana were both new to talking in each other's heads. The only way of finding out, however, demanded either a visit to one of his vampire friends or a trip to the Blood Bank. Foley would surely tell him all about this particular skill while gloating over the fact that Diana had ditched him.

Ryder was even more sure that Foley would leap at the chance to advance his own relationship with Diana. She called to men like one of the sirens of old with her enigmatic blend of vulnerability and strength. Not that Ryder blamed him. Diana's enticing darkness surrounded a pure heart. The way she still called to him.

He hated that. Hated how he ached for her. How he cared about her, despite his vow to stay away.

Her head tilted upward, rebellious in its posture. Her eyes, those amazing gold-green eyes, glittered with a hard light. And when the detective hugged her, she held on to him, her head buried against his chest.

Ryder was tempted to leap down there and…

What? he asked himself. The demon within—the one he had kept at bay for so long—answered all too quickly.

He would rip the other man's throat out with glee, not even bothering to slake his thirst afterward.

Fists clenched, Ryder battled the urge to do just that. He battled the feeling of power that surged through him when the demon emerged. That sense of might always threatened to corrupt his humanity. But he had allowed himself to explore his demon half because the vampire's strength let him help others. Let him be her hero.

But she had turned to others in her time of need and not to him.

Possibly never to him again.

Sorrow, raw and demanding, ripped through his heart.

He had almost been prepared for this anguish, as sharp and eviscerating as it was. Before Diana had made her request for space and time apart, he had known he should let her go. She deserved a real life before death called for her.

Now the slam of her car door reverberated in the silence of the early morning.

Ryder watched her car move away until a ray of sun sliced through a gap in the clouds, reminding him that his outing this morning had been but a short gift of freedom. The clouds were breaking up in anticipation of a sunny winter day.

Time for him to decide whether he should leave her alone in her misery or join her there.

The walls of her apartment closed in on her like the silk-lined top of a casket. Each breath seemed harder than the next, maybe because with each one she battled the tears she didn't want to shed. If she gave in, they would become a never-ending torrent that would drain her dry.

But she told herself to breathe. In and out, in and out. Slowly. Methodically. Maybe with that simple act she could hang on long enough…

The tap on the windowpane finally registered.

Rising up on one elbow, she noted a shadow on the fire escape. A familiar shadow. *Ryder.*

He was here. Just feet away. She could be in his arms. Only…

Her emotions were too muddled tonight. Too conflicted. As vulnerable as she was, it would be a mistake to see him. A mighty big mistake.

Somehow that thought didn't communicate it-self to the rest of her as she slipped from bed and belted her robe tight. She opened the window to find him leaning against the edge of the fire escape railing.

"Are you okay?" His voice was low. The dim light from the sliver of moon hid his features, but she could picture them in her mind. His dark eyes nearly gone black with emotion. Sharply defined brows drawn together in question.

"I've been better," she confessed.

"Is there anything I can do?"

She found herself sliding her leg up and over the sill. But she didn't go to him, choosing to remain close to the window, her back braced on one edge of the sash. Her legs crossed in front of her, but with her knees drawn up tight to her chest. She told herself it was because of the chill of the winter night and not to avoid touching him.

"I feel…" she began, her voice tight as the tears she had dammed up swelled, threatening to spill over. With a deep, quavery breath, she continued, "I feel like I failed…my dad. Sylvia. You."

Ryder didn't need the moonlight to see her face. Vampire sight illuminated the way she gripped her lower lip with her teeth, worrying it, the sheen of tears as they tracked down her face.

She must have realized she was crying for she suddenly buried her face against her knees.

That's when he did what she likely feared the most—he picked her up with his greater strength and cradled her in his lap.

She finally released a deluge of tears.

She gripped his shirt and sank her head against his chest. She sobbed until she collapsed against him, her body trembling from the violence of the release.

"I'm sorry." She shook her head dejectedly.

Ryder stroked his hand along her hair, down to her jaw. "There's no need to apologize."

"But there is. I asked you to leave. I can't expect you to show up here whenever—"

"I came of my own volition, darlin'."

This was wrong, Diana thought. How could she ever have a normal life if she gave in to her need for him whenever he came around? Especially now when she was unprepared and unwilling for this to go any further. But she needed an anchor. Something stable to stop the way her world was spinning out of control.

But Ryder couldn't be that anchor tonight. She was still too uncertain of her feelings for him and for a life filled by things other than death and mayhem. And vampires, both good and bad.

She must have tensed, because he asked, "What's wrong?"

She answered him frankly, wanting everything out in the open. "When my father died, I lost it. I let myself slip into…a bad place. The things I did. To myself. To Sebastian. To the other people I cared about…"

"But you left that world, Diana. You had the strength to make something of yourself."

"I thought I'd left that world. And then I met you." She placed her hand over his chest, rubbed it back and forth as she added, "Like you slip into your human skin when beneath—"

"There's the demon who doesn't want to play nice."

She nodded. "Maybe that's what brought us together. That twisted piece inside us that we can both barely control."

"That's not what it is, but you're too afraid to admit the truth."

The truth? She didn't know what that was. "I know you want—"

"For you to be happy, darlin'. I want that more than anything."

"I want the same for you. Only—"

He placed his finger on her lips to silence her. "You don't need to say it."

No, she didn't. They both understood their happiness might lie on separate paths.

"How do you handle it? Losing everyone and everything you know?"

His body stiffened beside hers and although he didn't say the words, she somehow knew. He had dealt with it much as she had—by putting up a wall around part of himself. By never letting anyone into that safe place.

"You stopped caring. You shut yourself off from the world."

"Like you did, darlin'. Only…that's not living. It's just surviving."

But retreating had helped her temper her hurt. Had let her function.

"Sometimes you have to embrace the darkness before you can get on with life," he said.

She met his gaze then, so intense and compelling. Filled with so much darkness.

"It's not always pain between us," Ryder said.

He cradled her jaw, offering solace with that touch.

"Isn't it?" she countered. "What do I bring you but the prospect of loss? Of watching me—"

She couldn't finish as he covered her mouth with his hand. "Don't. Please."

He could silence her physically, but not completely. *I can't bring you such pain.*

"Do you think leaving me now is any less painful?"

She shook her head, dislodging his hand from her mouth, but when she gazed up at him, he had morphed. His glowing eyes pierced the night, drawing her into their depths. Reminding her of what she would give up if she left him for good. The passion they could share forever.

The call of that promise…

Was sometimes too tempting. Like now, when she was so weak. So confused. When death had touched her life and made her wonder what it would be like to never die.

Except that she couldn't imagine living forever. She couldn't imagine seeing everyone around her die. Or fearing something as simple and beautiful as a sunrise. But she also couldn't imagine how Sylvia had spent those last moments of life. Had she suffered? Had she wanted more time?

Will I when it is my turn to die?

I would never take advantage of your fears, he said, returning to his human state.

You just did. She moved away from him. "I have to go. I need to be ready for tomorrow."

Tomorrow she was going to help Peter with the investigation in what little free time she had. The day would demand her total concentration.

So she slipped back inside her apartment and shut him out of her mind and, she hoped, out of her heart.

Chapter 6

She had missed the Blood Bank.

During the past year Stacia had been visiting with vampire friends in other cities. San Francisco. Miami. London. Amsterdam. Rome. Ah, Roma. The city of her birth and her death. As much as she had loved sampling the many fine young men and women lingering in the cafés around the Piazza Navona, New York City always felt like home.

Now she was back. And eager to catch up on all she'd missed—like the striking man crossing the room. Broad shoulders arrogantly thrust back, hips moving with a confident swagger, he made female heads turn. He exuded sex and danger— and something else, as well. Something that would make puny mortals quake with fear if they knew—he was a vampire. Like her.

Though, not exactly like her. He was much younger and his power was not so great. And the veneer of his humanity was still shiny and new, like the gleam of a freshly minted coin. But the shine of that humanity would rub away eventually. It would become tarnished the more he gave in to the beast within him. But for now...

"Delicious."

Her companion shot a look over his shoulder and shook his head ruefully. "Trust me, Stacia. Ryder is not interested. He's involved with a human."

She scoffed. "Why waste the time? Humans all die."

"Doesn't he know it. His lil' chit's best friend was just murdered."

She considered the comment. "So how can his human chit expect to satisfy him?"

Blake playfully nudged her shoulder with his. "Diana satisfies him with something you know nothing about—love."

Love. An oft-mentioned but thoroughly useless emotion after nearly two millennia of existence. She had believed in love, long ago, but time had taught her the futility of such an emotion. The loss that came with it, especially when it involved a human…she was immune to such pain by now.

But not to the need for passion. Especially with a handsome man such as that one. Of course, her current drinking partner was no slouch himself.

She cradled Blake's cheek and brushed her face against his. "So you don't think I know anything about love? Would you care to be proven wrong?"

He met her gaze. "It's not love with you, Stacia. It's sex."

"And that would be bad because…" She licked the shell of his ear and enjoyed the shudder that worked through his body.

"It would be bad because you elders drain vamps like me just for sport." He angled his body away from hers.

Annoyed and amused, she sent a little wave of power over him. His body reacted, a frisson of acknowledgment that rippled over his lean muscles. "Please, Stacia—"

"Begging, love?" She increased the strength of her power and commanded, "Touch me."

In her mind she formed a picture of what she wanted. A moment later he cupped her breast.

But it wasn't enough. It never seemed to be enough, she thought as she imagined him slipping his hand beneath her clothing.

He did as she fantasized, the cold of his palm bringing her nipple to a hard peak. But even as he moaned, he pleaded. "Stacia, this isn't what—"

"You want?" But *she* wanted it. She needed him to satisfy the emptiness inside of her. An emptiness sprung from being an elder, one of the vampires so old and powerful that none would challenge them. One of the vampires who had lost nearly every trace of their humanity.

Heady with her control over him and with the way his hand at her breast had her insides twisting for more, she stroked the magnificent erection in his lap.

"Take this to the back," Foley said, interrupting their interlude.

She looked past Blake's shoulder to where the bar owner waited, his eyes glimmering with lust. His intrusion angered her. With a wave of her hand, she sent punishment his way.

He grabbed his throat, struggling for air as she mentally disciplined him while still stroking Blake. While Blake continued to fondle her.

Sex and power. Power and death. A heady combination, she thought as Foley began to drop. Just a few minutes more and he'd be gone. Then something stopped her. Certainly not her conscience. Maybe the prospect of wasting time when she would much rather be riding Blake.

With another wave of her hand, she released Foley and increased her control over Blake. "Are you ready, love?"

"Devil take me, but I am," he said and followed her to one of the back rooms.

In the last few weeks, the vamps at his club had helped Ryder stop thinking about Diana. Or almost stop. And after an uneventful evening at the Blood Bank last night, he was eager for their company.

His friend Diego sat at the bar sipping a glass of wine. A usual pastime ever since the death of his lover, Esperanza.

Ryder clapped the other vampire on the back in greeting. "What are you up to, old man?"

Diego shot him a rueful glance. "Drowning my sorrows. Care to join me?"

He waved for another round of drinks. "It's

been quite a few months now, Diego. While I don't mind the way you're fattening my bank account by buying all these drinks—"

"*Mi amigo,* all wounds heal differently," he said, raising his head in a regal gesture and finished his last few sips of wine.

Ryder peered over Diego's shoulder to a group of young women congregated at the end of the bar, tittering and flirtatiously glancing their way. The signals were broadcasting loudly, only Diego wasn't picking them up.

"Maybe it's time for you to consider it, my friend."

Diego only shot a quick peek at the women before offering a toast to Ryder. "*Salud, amor y pesetas.*"

He picked up his glass, but paused before clinking it with the other vampire's. "Translation, *por favor.*"

Diego's crystal-blue eyes were vacant of all emotion except one—sorrow. "Health, love and money. I guess two out of three isn't so bad, is it?"

"No, *amigo.* Two of three is generally not so bad."

"What a pathetic bunch we have here," he

heard from behind him, and suddenly another vampire slipped an arm around him and Diego.

Blake popped his head into the space between the two of them. "Evenin', mates. Thought I'd drop by for a nip of something."

Diego muttered, "Wonderful. My insufferable night just got more insufferable."

"Come now, mate. Still lost in your cups? Maybe a good bite will—"

Blake didn't get to finish as Diego grabbed Blake's arm. "Mate," the older vampire said with some anger and an obvious hint of fang, "don't think that I will tolerate your stupidity even if you did help save my life not too long ago."

Ryder softly said, "Let him go, Diego. I can't have this kind of thing in my club."

With an apologetic nod, Diego did as asked.

Blake took a step away and rubbed his arm. "I was just trying to help."

"Because you are doing so well in the romance department?" Diego turned toward the bar once more and picked up his glass.

Ryder offered a drink to the younger, platinum-haired vampire who eagerly accepted it. He had no idea how Blake survived. As far as Ryder knew, Blake had no keeper and not enough money to pay for his blood. Which might account for why on occasion, Blake had indulged in a bite or two down at the Blood Bank. Maybe even why he had drained the young coed who was now the Lair's bartender to the point where he had to either turn Meghan or let her die.

"Thanks, mate. I'm a bit short of cash tonight," Blake said.

Ryder motioned for another drink and offered Blake the seat next to Diego. The young vampire refused, choosing instead to stand, glass held loosely in his hand.

"How is Meghan?" Blake asked, searching for any sign of the young vampire he'd sired.

Meghan was another regular at the Lair and she sometimes filled in for absent staff, but Ryder suspected she would stay away as long as she sensed the punk vampire's presence. A wonderful thing, this vamp radar. Good for either avoiding or tracking those you cared about.

"She's doing well. And you?" Ryder had seen the punk in and around the club on various occasions, but this was the first time he'd had the opportunity to speak with him since the incident months earlier that had endangered his new undead friends and had proved fatal for Diego's lover.

"Completely recovered, thanks. And you?"

"Fine." Although he was anything but. Otherwise he wouldn't be drinking with two vampires instead of with… "Fine," he repeated, more curtly.

Blake motioned to Ryder with his glass. "In this undead life, there's only one thing that could be responsible for that kind of attitude—a woman or the lack of one."

Diego turned on his stool and snarled, "Is this your new occupation—Dear Abby to lovelorn vampires? If so, you'd best find another. You suck at it."

Blake took another sip of his wine, considering Diego. When he finally spoke, some of his bravado was gone, as was his Cockney accent. "When I was a young lad, before I got turned, my sisters would always come to me with their problems. They thought I was a good listener."

"You had sisters who actually talked to you?" Diego asked.

"Two older and two younger, along with three younger brothers."

"*Mi hermanita* was headstrong. My mother swore my sister would make her gray before her time," Diego replied with a wistful smile on his face.

"Did she?" Ryder asked. He'd been an only child and had never had the pleasure of a family with his wife.

A flash of sorrow flickered across Diego's face. "She died of a fever before she could."

"I lost a sister that way, too," Blake commiserated, and laid a hand on Diego's shoulder.

"And the rest?" Diego asked with an arch of his brow.

"Going hungry with the famine when I…" Blake couldn't continue and Ryder didn't want him to. He'd been feeling morose enough without this discussion about death and loved ones. The theme struck too close to home tonight.

"Gentlemen, as Blake noted, we are a sorry lot and sitting here in our cups is accomplishing nothing."

"And what do you propose, *amigo?*"

"Yeah, wot?" Blake asked, reverting to his punk self.

Ryder smiled, suddenly knowing just what

might relieve some of the unpleasantness of the night. "Time to let loose, don't you think?"

With that, he motioned to his friends to step outside. Once in the small alley, he reached within and woke the beast. Without Diana, he could summon and dismiss the vampire when he desired. It was only around her that his control grew spotty, evidenced by the fact that he'd put the bite on her twice now. The second time, he had nearly been unable to stop, overcome by passion.

Heat flared to life at the remembrance of that night. His fangs burst from his mouth. As he faced his friends, his voice was low and held the rumble of the stirring animal. "Let's go."

He didn't know how long it had been, only that he was panting, his body burning with undead power as they settled on the roof of the building across from the Blood Bank. They must have covered most of Manhattan in their flight over rooftops and through the park, reveling in the physical freedom that came from releasing their demons.

For so long Ryder had denied that the animal

brought him anything other than disgust. Only recently had he made any effort to understand it or to acknowledge that his darkness could be used for good.

"I'm a mite thirsty," Blake said, his shoulders visibly rising as he tried to slow his breathing. He tucked his black T-shirt back into his jeans and straightened his black leather jacket.

"As am I." Not a piece of Diego's elegant attire was out of place, unlike Ryder and Blake.

Ryder repaired his clothing then plummeted over the edge of the building to the earth below. He barely heard the soft thuds of his companions as they joined him on the alley's cobblestones. At the door of the club, he hesitated, but something compelled him forward. Not the demon, but the human in him who wanted to confirm that even when he was surrounded by the undead, his mortal self still dominated.

The bouncer granted them entry and once inside, the essence of others like them greeted him. At the far end of the club, Foley talked to a petite, dark-haired woman. A familiar silhouette, clad in black leather that fit like a second skin.

Violence rose up inside of Ryder and the beast

nearly overwhelmed him with its desire to exact punishment on the other vampire. Ryder clenched his fists. So much for restraint, he thought as he stepped toward the couple.

Diego snared his arm. "It's not who you think."

"Open your senses, mate. She's one of the elders." Blake stepped up to Ryder's back and placed a hand on his shoulder to check him.

Taking a breath, Ryder released the restraints on his animal. Suddenly, the surge of power coming off the female rippled through him, telling him she was not only undead, but as Blake had said, quite old and powerful. The strength of her energy swirled about her and spilled out into the crowd. Chum for vamps, he thought. How many did she attract with her deadly bait?

"Easy, *mi amigo*. She's not to be taken lightly," Diego warned, but Ryder had no way to suppress the experience of her.

Painfully he stood there, poised on the edge of…anticipation, both sexual and intellectual. What could this vamp be like that she had so much sway without his even knowing her name, without his having seen her face?

She turned then, and energy surged through

him, singeing his senses. The force of her acknowledgment was so strong he had to rein in the
beast before it rushed to her side. Control, after
all, being one of his goals.

She smiled at him, as if amused by his struggle. She approached, a sex-filled sway in her
hips that promised oblivion between her long,
leather-clad legs.

Dipping her head to one side, she barely
glanced at his two friends. "Diego. Blake." She
examined him. "And you are?"

"Ryder Latimer," he answered, fascinated by
her appearance, so much like Diana's. Dark,
nearly seal-black hair cropped close to her head
exposed the perfect curves of her ears, which
were adorned with an assortment of golden rings.
Her brows were smudges of black against pale
skin. One brow was threaded with a golden ring
that shifted with her brow as she raised it in
amusement.

"Intrigued?" She motioned to Blake and
Diego. "Leave us."

"He's not like the rest of us, Stacia," Diego
said, which only earned him a chuckle from the
very attractive vamp.

"Of course not. That's what makes him so interesting."

That she could so blithely ignore Diego confirmed one thing—she obviously possessed more power. Her intense force coupled with her apparent rashness made her formidable. From the rumors Ryder had heard from his friends, the elders were old, powerful and brutal.

"More interesting than me, luv?" Blake asked.

She smiled and walked to the upstart vamp.

"Ah, Blake. The other night was wonderful." She laid a hand on Blake's chest and his face filled with…

Ryder couldn't tell if fear or passion ruled. She trailed her finely boned hand up to Blake's jaw then playfully tousled his pale white hair. Blake moaned with unfulfilled desire.

Stacia laughed sexily. "Always the randy young pup. That's good. Maybe you and I can get together again later, but now…" She slipped her arm through Ryder's. "I'd like to know more about you, Ryder."

Chapter 7

For most of her life, Diana had suffered from nightmares featuring demons and dying. She had never figured out what caused them or why they had ended once she'd become involved with Ryder. She suspected the existence of real monsters proved scarier than the stuff of her dreams.

After visiting Sylvia's office a few days ago, however, her sleep had once again been plagued by visions—of Sylvia lying dead on the M.E.'s table and of her dad and of Ryder.

She could understand the connection between Sylvia and her *papi*, two loved ones taken from her well before their time. As for Ryder's appearance—she wrote that off to her conflicting emotions about his role in her life and to the reality that Ryder had already cheated death. Because of his near immortality, he had dealt with the loss of so many of his loved ones and somehow survived. In some twisted way, that gave her the confidence that she, too, could survive this distressing episode and eventually return to a more normal life.

A visit to Sylvia's office had provided information key to the investigation—the name of a Nervous Nelly client Sylvia had seen shortly before her death. Arturo de la Fuente had normally been the client of Sylvia's partner, Steve Martinez. The request to meet with Sylvia had been out of the ordinary. Because of that, they'd visited de la Fuente and discovered a ledger that pointed to a money-laundering scheme. Finally they had a motive for her friend's murder other than a husband's jealous rage.

In the days since that discovery, Diana and her partner had assembled a team to investigate the money laundering since that crime was within the FBI's jurisdiction. They had also defined the boundaries of their probe with Daly and his squad so as to not interfere with the ongoing search to find Sylvia's killer.

Sleepless nights combined with getting everything coordinated at work had stolen a great deal of her time and energy. She was exhausted, both

Death Calls

mentally and physically. As she stepped inside her apartment she could only listen to the silence. Her home was devoid of any signs of life. Darkness swallowed her up.

As empty as the apartment seemed at times, the loneliness of it was what she needed. Space to confirm whether what she truly wanted was happily-ever-after with a mortal man or a life with Ryder.

It had been weeks since she'd left him and she still didn't know. Maybe she never would.

She quickly prepped for sleep and slipped beneath the sheets. She hugged the pillow next to her and inhaled deeply, recalling the scent of him, the cold of his skin that quickly fled at her touch—a touch that often roused the vampire and brought both fear and fascination on her part.

With a sigh, she tossed the pillow away and chastised herself. She had to be strong enough to let him go, and to truly try to find out what it was she wanted from her life.

She had to decide if the course she had chosen was the right one. The one that would finally make her happy.

* * *

Ryder hadn't known what to expect from the ancient vampiress the night before. Certainly not the charming creature who had blithely dismissed close to two thousand years of existence as if it was nothing.

Millennia of life. Millennia of loss. That was all Ryder thought about when he should have been working on the club's ledgers. That, and Diana.

While it had been difficult to acquiesce to Diana's request for time apart, he had done so. First because he wanted her to be happy. Even if that happiness didn't include him. Second because he'd had time to more freely explore his demon side—the side that scared and fascinated her much as it did him.

Humans were born to die, he reminded himself. Unless of course…

What would he do if Diana did return to him? Could he be by her side and watch her grow old? When the time came and only a moment remained to her life would her last breath be his name? Would she ask him to turn her? And if she didn't, could he restrain the beast—and the human—who feared being alone again?

In his dreams, or maybe it was more correct to call them nightmares, he had imagined Diana's death. He'd imagined the look in her eyes, shock that death had called, fear that time was almost gone.

In his dreams, he lowered his head to her neck and sank his fangs through the fragile skin. He bit deeply and sucked her nearly dry before offering up his tainted blood to grant her near immortality.

Would she hate him afterward the way he had hated the woman who had turned him?

Maybe that was what had fascinated him about Stacia—her calm acceptance of her fate, of her power.

Would he have similar strength one day? Would he have the kind of control that she possessed, not only over lesser vampires, but over herself? Despite what he'd heard about the elders, Stacia still possessed her humanity. Or at least, a small token of it.

His powers and those of his friends paled in comparison to what he detected deep beneath Stacia's visibly composed exterior. How he knew that, he was uncertain. Maybe it was some undead thing he had yet to understand, some protective barometer that existed to warn him when he was outvamped. Not that he was heeding that warning any more than he listened to those voiced by Diego and Blake. His two friends had spent a good part of the night telling him not to underestimate Stacia.

Fascination with the elder vampire tempted him to return to the Blood Bank, but look where giving in to Diana's appeal had gotten him. So he forced himself to stay at the Lair long after he'd reviewed the books and dealt with all the daily needs of running his establishment and long after the music below told him the club was open for business.

When he allowed himself to leave his office, it was after two in the morning, close to closing. Just a dozen or so stragglers were being chased out.

Nothing of interest and no unwanted visitors. And then Stacia walked in, dressed in all that sinful black leather. It made her fair skin even more striking against the darkness of her hair.

Her wave of power crashed over him again. But he still had the presence of mind to think it a shame her skin didn't have the healthy tanned splendor of Diana's and that her eyes—almond-shaped like those of his ex-lover—were dark and absent the spark of life in Diana's golden-green gaze.

Shaking his head to drive both women out of his mind, he approached her. She looked surprised. Did she think he feared her?

"I wasn't expecting you," he said.

Obviously not enough of a greeting for her. She stood on tiptoe and whispered in his ear, "I didn't think you'd come back to me willingly."

As she retreated, she brushed a kiss along the side of his face, which sent a shiver through him. He wasn't sure if it was one of desire or revulsion. Her breath smelled of fresh blood and the warmth in her skin said she had recently fed. But not a lot. Her skin lacked the colorful blush that came with a full feeding.

A part of him was intrigued by that. It confirmed that she had dominion over her demon and, possibly, some semblance of humanity lurking within her ancient heart.

He tucked his hands into the pockets of his pants and narrowed his eyes. "Why are you here, Stacia?"

Once again she seemed taken aback, as if she

couldn't believe he was capable of resisting her charms. "You interest me. That's not an easy thing to do."

The feeling was decidedly mutual. Stacia's long existence and her apparent ability to deal with it made him wonder what he could learn from her.

That she sensed his curiosity was obvious from her pleased smile. "So what do we do about this?"

"Care for a drink?" He held his hand out in the direction of the bar. "Nothing illegal," he clarified.

"That's a shame." She walked past him, brushing her body against his in a way that warned she wanted more than just talk.

This *was* going to be fascinating, he thought, and a second later he heard in his head, *It certainly will be, my beloved.*

Chapter 8

Ryder's absence from her life had provided an unexpected boon to her investigation on Sylvia's murder—last night's sleeplessness had allowed Diana to review the reports her team had assembled.

De la Fuente's import/export business had funneled money to more than a dozen companies with one fascinating connection. All of the fake corporations had been created based on the instructions of a partner at Sylvia's law firm—none other than Steve Martinez.

In time, Diana would make sure that Martinez paid for his role in her friend's murder. She wouldn't allow anyone to plea bargain the case or to grant Martinez immunity. In the back of her mind came the unbidden thought that in Ryder's world, as grim and uncivilized as it might be at times, there would be no hesitation about meting out the right brand of justice.

For the moment, however, her main goal was to track down de la Fuente so that she would have the evidence she needed to make her case.

Which was why she and David were on their way to Spanish Harlem and de la Fuente's office. The area was predominantly Latino, a mix of Newyoricans and Dominicans, the Dominicans prevailing in number.

She and David left their car and walked to a small *bodega* where a few older men sat in front, playing dominoes. She never got a chance to pull out her badge.

"*Niña.* We know who you are," one man said, slapped a domino down on the table and gestured for the man next to him to make a move.

That man hesitated. She looked over his shoulder at the dominoes he held in his large grizzled hand. Bending, she whispered, *"El nueve."*

With but a quick look at the table, the man nodded, fitted the nine domino to one end and displayed his hand—a winning one.

"*Chica,* that wasn't nice. Ricky would never have gotten that on his own."

She smiled and tucked her hands behind her back. "*Bueno,* here's how it is. I can stand here all day playing dominoes or you can answer a few questions so I can leave."

The choice of all of the men, except for Ricky, was clear. She quickly fired off a series of questions in Spanish and received the answers she needed. When she thanked the men and began to walk away, David asked, "What's up?"

"Besides you needing Spanish lessons, *mi amigo?*"

"Maggie's taught me plenty of Spanish. Taco. Salsa. *Amorcito.* And for those special moments, *Co*—"

She held up her hand to keep him from muttering her most commonly used curse word. "I get it. We're heading to Second Avenue. Artie keeps a love nest there with his assistant."

As she walked past the store next to the *bodega,* she paused. In the windows were all kinds of Latino specialties, from the familiar Cuban sandwiches to cheese-filled arepas, courtesy of the Colombian influence in the neighborhood. The area reminded her of Calle Ocho in Miami, where she had lived as a small girl before the

Reyes's had moved up and out to the Miami suburbs.

But she had no time to ponder the feelings those memories inspired. She hurried her pace, eager to reach the apartment building off Second where the men had said she might find de la Fuente. She and David had just turned the corner of the block when she noticed none other than Arturo de la Fuente.

He had taken no more than a few steps when the door of a parked car flew open. A large man jumped out and blocked his way.

She ran beside David, no doubt in her mind as to who would take which suspect. The man from the car was at least six feet tall with the muscular build of a Mr. Olympia. She would be like a gnat swarming an ox if she went for him. De la Fuente, however, was just right. Pencil-thin. Petite. Dog meat, she thought as she and David raced toward the men.

Mr. Olympia had nearly shoved de la Fuente into the waiting car when David tackled him to the ground, freeing de la Fuente. She clotheslined the man as he tried to run past. Once he was on the ground, she quickly flipped him and with a knee smack in the middle of his back, cuffed one hand and slipped the other cuff over the handle of a parked car.

By the time she got to her feet, her partner had restrained the muscular man and was headed toward the getaway car.

The man behind the wheel raised his hand.

The adage about seeing your life flash in front of your face came to mind, only it was David's life in her vision. David being shot. Going down. She imagined explaining to Maggie what had happened. How he had died.

She couldn't let it happen.

Launching herself at her partner, she knocked him out of the line of fire.

The sound of gunfire echoed from the interior of the car followed by the screech of tires.

She cursed and looked at her partner. David rubbed his side.

"Shit, Reyes. You are one bony thing," he teased.

She couldn't let it go. He'd almost gotten killed. She couldn't imagine being at his side and watching him die.

Like Ryder might watch you die one day?

With anger and fear overriding everything else, she grabbed his suit jacket and body-slammed him against the side of a parked car. "Don't ever do anything stupid like that again unless you don't want to continue being my partner."

"As if I like being your partner. You're domineering. Aggressive. Hot-tempered."

The tension of the moment fled with his ever-calm demeanor and the teasing note in his voice.

"You do know how to turn a girl's head." But she shoved him against the car again just for good measure.

"Of course I want to keep being your partner. You make life…interesting."

"Then you will never do something stupid like that again."

She whirled from him to fetch de la Fuente.

"Going soft on me?" he teased, but they both got back to the business at hand—bringing in these two suspects and locating the one that had unfortunately gotten away.

Peter Daly met them at FBI headquarters and they headed to the interrogation room holding Max Moreno—Mr. Olympia.

"Want to tell us what part you had in the murder of Sylvia Rodriguez?" Diana asked.

"I don't know what you're talking about. Artie owed me some cash and I was trying to collect." Max leaned back in the chair, trying to appear unruffled by his incarceration, but the scared tone of his voice was apparent to all.

"You understand that we've got you on a kidnapping charge at a minimum. If your friends are up to anything else, you're going down for that, as well." She assumed a very casual stance. "You got kids, Max?"

The look on his face provided the answer she needed and she continued. "Think what it'll be like, not being with them for…let's say, the next twenty or thirty years."

A slight tremor echoed through Max's posture. "You can't prove a thing."

Diana pointed to Peter. "Do you think both the N.Y.P.D. and FBI were watching your friend Artie because they couldn't prove anything? We've got messages, trails of money. A lot more, Max."

They didn't have all of that yet, but it was only a matter of time before they did. They had already put in a request to use the National Security Agency's Echelon system to start tracking things and they were employing their own Carnivore program to round up any e-mails.

Max looked at David and tried to fake bravado. "You let a woman do all the talking for you?"

"Let it go, Diana. This guy's obviously too stupid to see he's already a casualty in this war," David said with no hint of anger or anything besides sheer boredom.

Knowing he was adopting the role they used during their standard interrogations, she followed him and Peter into the hall.

David said, "I'm getting a bad feeling about this."

"I totally agree," Peter said. "Moreno and the friend who got away were just foot soldiers. But when you have soldiers, you have a general. By the way, the license plate you called in—the car was stolen this morning."

David glanced at her uneasily. "What now?"

"We keep questioning Artie and Max. See where that leads."

"First, I'm going to get some java. Want some?" Peter asked.

"You bet. A *venti*—"

"*Caramel macchiato.* You're so predictable, Reyes. Anything for you, Harris?"

David shook his head and watched Peter walk away. "Is there something going on between you two?"

"Just friends," she answered quickly as she walked to her office under David's close examination. "Peter's a nice guy, but—"

"You're still involved with—"

She held up her hand to silence him. "Say the name and die."

He laughed. "Well, I guess that tells me all I need to know. Call me when you're ready to start the interrogation again."

Diana watched David enter his office and wished that forgetting Ryder could be as easy as refusing to say his name. She hadn't seen him since the night of the funeral—at least, not in person. But he had been in her dreams. She didn't know what was worse—having him up close and personal and making her afraid of what she was feeling, or giving in to him in her nighttime fantasies and experiencing mind-blowing lovemaking.

Until he put the bite on her, then reality flew back at her, reminded her of why she had broken it off with him. What she felt with him…it wasn't normal.

But, *Dios mio,* what it did…

Her body tightened and she fought to keep her reaction under control.

She sat at her desk and tried to concentrate on the de la Fuente file, only her mind was too busy thinking about the feel of Ryder's mouth on her skin. The slight pain as he bit through it. The heat that spread throughout her body as he drank her blood.

She had to have something wrong with her that she was now wondering if she should have left him.

She had no desire to become one of the undead. While a life without end held appeal for some people, she wasn't sure she could handle it. She had barely handled her father's death. And now she was doing only a little better with Sylvia's. She tried to imagine what it would be like to lose the rest of the loved ones in her life—her mother and Sebastian, Melissa and the baby she carried, Maggie, David.

She couldn't deal with it. And she had no right to inflict that kind of suffering on Ryder, either. She couldn't make him watch her die.

But could she spend the rest of her life without the kind of passion he roused?

Breathing a disgusted sigh, she chastised herself for her uncertainty. Uncertainty brought weakness. And weakness brought failure.

She couldn't afford to fail. Not Sylvia or herself.

Chapter 9

"Is it true, then?" Foley asked with a sharp smile as he delivered shots for Ryder and Diego. "Is your delectable Diana free for—"

In a millisecond, Ryder had Foley's throat in his hand, gripped so tightly that he heard the crunch of cartilage beneath his fingers. He lifted the other vamp nearly over the bar.

Somehow Foley managed to choke out, "She's yours. All yours." He hissed something else, something unintelligible, with what little breath he had left.

Suddenly a small hand grasped Ryder's arm and applied pressure. "Beloved, he's not worth the effort."

Ryder released Foley, who crab-walked away from them as quickly as he could, and he turned to Stacia. With her vanity, she had mistakenly believed the exchange to be about her. Sensing that she wouldn't take kindly to knowing otherwise, he said, "I wasn't expecting you."

Stacia cupped his cheek. Her palm was cold against his skin. She traced the edges of his lips and her thumb came away stained with a remnant of his snack. She snaked her tongue out to lick it off. "Delicious." The look in her hungry eyes made it clear that she wasn't referring to the blood.

"Subtlety has never been your strong suit," Diego said with a harsh snicker.

She wasn't about to let the slight go unnoticed.

She slipped an arm around Diego's waist and morphed, her eyes going from their normally dark hue to an almost phosphorescent blue-green. Her fangs burst from her mouth, sharp, white and lethally long. At least a few inches. Far longer than Ryder's or Diego's. Another sign of vamp age? Was this what long in the tooth meant?

His amusement fled when she reached up and jerked Diego's head to the side, exposing his vulnerable neck.

"You remember, *amor,* don't you?" she asked, her tone filled with the dual promise of passion and violence.

She grazed Diego's neck with her teeth, breaking the skin just enough to draw blood. Diego shivered and moaned with need.

Ryder felt the energy pulse from her body and envelop his friend. As Stacia flicked a glance in his direction, the field of power expanded and he experienced the pull Stacia exerted over Diego as surely as if it was his neck she was now licking with slow, catlike strokes.

Stacia placed one final lick on Diego's neck, but as she did so, her dark gaze locked with Ryder's. "Care to join us?"

Ryder peered at the ancient vamp, battling the images that suddenly flashed through his mind of all that she planned to do to his friend in one of the back rooms. Violence mixed with passion so intense, it pulled an arousal from him—not just of the beast but of the human. Summoning his waning willpower, he said, "I never was much for threesomes."

Stacia smiled, displaying those decidedly dangerous fangs. "Even better, beloved. I'll wait to have you all to myself."

She strode away, Diego beside her. Petite shoulders pulled back confidently, reflecting surety in her eventual possession of him. He wondered what Stacia would do if he confessed that no matter how attractive she was, his mind invariably returned to another dark and petite dominatrix.

One named Diana.

Her night had been restless, filled not only with dreams of Ryder but with an unsettling sense that their connection was weakening. Even before he had bitten her, there had been some kind of link between them. With each bite, that connection had grown stronger. What she hadn't realized until recently was that no matter how far apart they were, she still felt him. Until lately.

The growing chasm between them sat heavily on her mind, so hard to ignore that it kept her awake and made her head to work early.

Surprisingly, she got beeped by her Assistant Director in Charge as she cleared security. She was needed immediately and wasted no time in rushing to the ADIC's office, where she ran into David.

ADIC Hernandez's curt response as he saw them provided no comfort. "Let's go."

He opened the door to reveal another man sitting in front of his desk. The man rose and turned, a simple act, and yet raw threat came off of him in waves.

"This is Agent Henry Rupert from the CIA. He's here to discuss the de la Fuente case."

The older man pulled out his identification and flashed it, his movements brusque, possibly even resentful, she thought.

"Agent Rupert," she acknowledged with a nod of her head.

The CIA agent showed little emotion as he said, "Call me Hank since it seems as if we'll have to work together."

Diana listened patiently to her ADIC's briefing. It seemed that her investigation into the money-laundering scheme had unwittingly stepped on one being conducted by Rupert and the CIA into the theft of a weapon and its subsequent purchase by a domestic paramilitary group—the Cuban Democratic Army.

Agent Rupert struck her as a man of action and command, his manner as blunt as the tips of the Marine buzz-cut he favored. She pictured him charging bullishly ahead to achieve his objective.

She was surprised, therefore, that he sat calmly while ADIC Hernandez turned over command of the investigation to her since domestic terrorism was normally within the FBI's jurisdiction. Rupert would remain the key CIA contact and work with her and David as necessary.

As her ADIC finished with his speech about interagency cooperation, an oxymoron if there ever was one, he motioned to Rupert. "Hank can fill you in on the specifics of the CIA investigation. I trust you and David can do the same regarding ours. Copies of the latest reports are in your office, Diana. At 9:00 a.m. tomorrow, we will have a meeting of the joint teams."

Diana bit back any objections. In the close to six years she had worked for the Bureau under Jesus Hernandez, she had found him to be a reasonable man who knew the right political moves. He had supported her on various cases and she respected him too much to challenge his decision. "We'll do the best that we can. Agent Rupert?"

Rupert exhaled a long, almost strangled breath. "Can't say I'm pleased, but I'll do what I have to."

Exasperation colored his words. He probably resented that she was younger, a woman and, more so, a Cubana. Maybe his pique had been responsible for that earlier sense of threat she'd perceived. Had the situations been reversed, she certainly would have been pissed off. She tried to smooth things over. "I think a man of your experience will help get things moving quickly. I'm looking forward to working together." She offered her hand.

After a long inspection that gave away nothing he was thinking, he shook her hand and then David's. "Let's get rolling. We have a lot to do before tomorrow morning."

Rupert strode out of the ADIC's office, obviously expecting them to follow his lead. Diana shoved her anger back. Rupert was likely used to being in command and she would give him that little bit…for now.

Diana leaned back and steepled her elbows on the arms of the chair as she considered Agent Rupert and his comments about the Cuban Democratic Army.

"Are you angry that we have to work together?" she asked, wanting everything out in the open.

Rupert shrugged and barely managed to fold his arms across his barrel chest. "Aren't you?"

"As a matter of fact, I am. My investigation was going well."

"As was mine." Each word was clipped. "We nailed a couple of CDA members."

"But clearly you didn't get exactly what you were after."

He smiled at her in recognition of the truth of her statement. "No, clearly not what we were after. Which leaves me here, uneasy allies with the FBI, trying to put an end to—" He stopped abruptly, clearly holding back.

David forced the issue by asking, "What are we trying to end, Agent Rupert?"

Exasperated with every second Rupert delayed, she sat up straighter in her chair and pointedly met Rupert's gaze. "Agent Rupert—"

"Hank. You two are young enough without making me feel older with all the sirs and 'Agent this and that,'" he replied.

"Hank," she began, unduly stressing his name. "This isn't going to work unless we get one hundred percent cooperation."

His gaze skittered from her to David. "My undercover source tells me the CDA plans to take down either the United Nations or the Cuban Mission on Lexington Avenue in order to call attention to Cuba's oppressive regime and pattern of human rights violations."

"Twisted logic," David said. "You trust this source?"

A shrewd smile spread across the older man's lips. "Your partner would know if he's trustworthy."

"Excuse me? How would I—"

She stopped when Rupert slid a file in front of her and a familiar face stared back—Alejandro Garcia. Son of a Bay of Pigs soldier and, from what she noted in the file, on special assignment from the Miami branch of the DEA.

But more importantly, Alejandro Garcia was her former boyfriend and lover. Her first love. The man she had once thought she would marry and have a family with.

Her Alex, she thought, sadly remembering how it had ended between them.

"Diana?" David questioned.

She gave the papers to her partner for review. "I've known Alejandro since elementary school."

"He was your high school sweetheart and college love."

"You've obviously done your homework, Hank. Why Alejandro for this assignment?"

Rupert shifted his fullback-wide shoulders in a careless shrug. "His father is as close as you can get to a local hero in Little Havana. Who better to infiltrate a group whose leader fancies one day ruling Cuba?"

"You suspect de la Fuente and Moreno are involved with this group?"

"Garcia has confirmed that Moreno's a CDA member. We know who's funding them—a Colombian drug cartel that's been wanting to expand. Now thanks to you, we know that de la Fuente got the money from them to the CDA."

"Why New York with all that's happened lately? The CDA must know we're on a heightened state of alert," David said, clearly ill at ease with the picture Rupert painted.

The older man shook his head. "They probably don't care since—"

"There are plenty of people who want to see a regime change in Cuba?" Did Rupert have doubts about her commitment given her background?

Rupert surprised her by losing his earlier artificially imposed nonchalance. "Tell me you don't want Cuba free, Reyes."

"Hear this, Hank," she said, although her use of his name was anything but friendly. "I'm going to stop this from happening. What you think about my community's politics doesn't matter a rat's ass. Besides, I have my own reasons."

There was a moment's pause on Rupert's part before he said, "A reason besides your friend? Like maybe the drug dealers that killed your father?"

Her head snapped back as if she'd been struck. "I guess you got your hands on my personal file, which prompts me to ask what other kinds of information you shadowy CIA types might have."

"Just what we need to do the job, Reyes." He had broken every rule in the book by looking at her file.

She eyed him with suspicion. "My psych profile and other *personal* information aren't in that category."

He grinned, but his eyes were cold and flat, like a snake's. "Well, you know what they say—know your friends, but know your enemies better."

"Are we your enemies, Agent Rupert?" David

sat on the edge of Diana's desk in an effort to provide a united front.

"Time will tell," Rupert said.

Chapter 10

If God laughed at women who made plans, she was sure He was rolling in the aisles right about now. She was sitting in a safe house in Union City, New Jersey, waiting for a visit from the CIA's deep cover operative Alejandro Garcia.

Her Alex.

David, with his infinite wisdom, had thought it wiser for Diana to meet Alex by herself and fill him in on the briefings after she settled whatever things she might need to settle with her ex.

Her ex.

At one time, Alex had been the center of her life. They'd fancied themselves getting married. Having kids. Doing all the normal things normal people do. Until the death of her father had changed all those plans.

Changed her.

Had it also changed Alex? What was his life like now? Was he married? Did he have children? Did he have all those things they had once dreamed of sharing together?

Unlike Rupert, she was not about to pull strings to get the answers. She wasn't even sure she deserved them considering how it had ended between them.

"Penny for your thoughts."

She had been so engrossed in her thoughts she hadn't heard him enter the apartment. After what seemed like forever, there he was, up close and personal.

"Alex." Her voice was husky with suppressed emotion.

He had aged a little, but who hadn't? Unbidden came the thought that he'd grown into a recklessly handsome man with his perfect smile and light green eyes. His body had filled out admirably with leanly defined muscle well served by the T-shirt and jeans he wore.

She stepped closer, hoping he hadn't noticed her perusal.

"Not glad to see me?"

Before she knew it, they were in each other's

arms, the embrace one of friendship and solace. One that seemed like a homecoming despite nearly a decade of separation.

"I'm sorry about Sylvia," he said when he finally stepped away.

"*Gracias.* I know she'll get justice with both of us on the case."

"*Sí.* Funny thing, both of us on this case. Both of us in law enforcement," he said.

A funny thing indeed, she thought. She motioned to the bag he'd put on the table. "As late as it is, I'm hoping that's dinner."

Alex smiled. "I haven't had a chance to eat, and figured your day might very well have been the same."

With a broad nod of her head, she said, "You guessed it."

"*Ropa vieja* still your favorite? With sides of *platanos maduros* and *tostones?*"

"You didn't forget the avocado salad, did you?" she asked, both surprised and touched that he had remembered her favorites.

"I could never forget." His eyes darkened to confirm that was not all he had not forgotten.

Slightly disquieted by that possibility, she inclined her head in the direction of the kitchen. "Care to have a working dinner?"

A touch of tension entered his smile, as if he sensed she was pushing him away. Again. "I'm not trying to pick up where we left off, because—"

"That would be impossible," she finished for him. Very impossible since she wasn't sure whether her heart was free at the moment.

"It would. We're very different people. Or at least, I am," he admitted as he walked over to the table and spread out the assorted take-out plates.

"I am, too, Alex." She joined him, but opted for removing papers from her briefcase, unsettled by the discussion.

"Diana, *mi amor.* You've still got your defenses up. I felt them the moment I walked in."

He had always been able to read her emotions, and the truth of it was, he was right. Her defenses were definitely on full-blast. "What I want most right now is to solve this case and get my life back on track."

"Sylvia's death having derailed you the way your dad's did?" The tone of his words held a strange mix of condemnation and concern.

Irritation flared to life, but she tamped it down. He, more than most, had a right to that censure. But it was time to move away from personal issues and on to more demanding ones. "Are you ready to go over what we have?"

A wry smirk flitted across his lips before he gestured to the table. She sat beside him and tried to recall his usual choices. They came to mind as if she was still standing at the noisy take-out counter at La Carreta on Calle Oche. *Bistec empanizado.* He usually got the chicken-fried steak with beans and rice. The dishes on his side of the table confirmed her recollection had been correct. At least she wasn't the only one still easy to read.

She ate some of the tender shredded beef swimming in tomato sauce. Flavorful and with just the right blend of spices. "*Delicioso.* As good as *mami's.*"

He chuckled as he flipped a page from the files. "Don't let her hear that." Before she could say anything else, he said, "Why don't you give me your impressions of the case?"

Although it was phrased as a request, there was no doubting the command behind his words. Interesting, she thought. Alex had rarely been the take-charge type. Nevertheless, she did as he asked, and he listened carefully as she explained how she and Peter Daly had unwittingly stumbled upon the money laundering and ended up nabbing Moreno and de la Fuente, as well.

"We tracked down a number of corporations receiving the money and making payments. Next was finding who actually deposited the money."

"There's a Colombian drug ring based in Corona. If we dig, we'll likely find that all the deposits were either done by them or other members of the CDA." Alex pointed out the pictures of the drug ring and CDA members from the file Hank Rupert had provided.

"A strange alliance. It's even stranger that with so much money going into de la Fuente's account, no one noticed," she said. Banks were supposed to carefully monitor such activities.

Alex shot her a skeptical look. "Didn't notice or maybe got paid not to?"

She shrugged, picked up a *tostone* from the plate and offered up the twice-fried plantain to him. Too much like old times, she thought. She would be wise not to fall into old habits. "Probably the latter, but there's nothing suspicious about the bank personnel. After de la Fuente's activities, the trail gets ice-cold. The dummy corporations' accounts were accessed via the Internet."

Alex snagged the plantain from her and chewed on it thoughtfully before replying. "The wonders of modern banking. From drug money to fully available e-money."

"Impossible to trace," she agreed. "So we know how they got the money."

She searched Alex's face. It showed no trace of emotion and yet her gut told her he was keeping something from her. Another new development in her ex-lover. He'd always been easy to read. "So why don't you tell me the why?"

He hesitated as he scooped up some of the rice and beans, the delay confirming her instinct hadn't failed her. "Hank's probably told you most of this." He had a hard glint in his eyes as he met her gaze.

A sick feeling settled into the pit of her stomach. For a moment she told herself she really didn't want to know the worst-case scenario. But only for a moment, since she knew that to solve this case, she needed all the information. "What else is there?"

He braced his forearms on the edge of the table. "Need to know only."

"My partner—"

"No one besides him and your ADIC. It's too risky. The weapon stolen from an army base was an experimental prototype for a hand-held smart bomb delivery system and the warheads for same."

"Ah, fresh destructive power from our wonderful military machine," she quipped to hide her unease. "Possible chemical, biological, radiological or nuclear kind of destruction?"

"Definitely convertible to a CBRN," Alex explained. "Although the warheads stolen were your garden variety explosives. But still capable of taking down a large building."

A shiver worked through her at the thought. She and David had barely managed to escape the collapse of the World Trade Center after going in to help survivors during the 9/11 attack.

"Diana?" He laid his hand over hers, clearly sensing her disquiet.

To her surprise, comfort filled her with that simple touch. "I'm okay. Go on, *por favor*."

"About three months ago, the CIA heard rumors of this prototype being up for grabs. They intercepted a flurry of e-mails and phone calls that seemed to indicate a purchase had been made."

He extracted one spreadsheet where her team had painstakingly documented various money transfers. He pointed to the last series of entries. "Right about this time."

Diana glanced quickly at the papers, already familiar with the story they told. "So the Colombian money goes to the militiamen to buy a very fancy piece of hardware."

Alex nodded. "Maybe too many deals gone sour with their contacts in Cuba or they feel that with a new regime, it'll be easier to run drugs."

"They think attacking the United Nations or the Cuban Mission will accomplish that?"

"Illogical, but extremists and logic don't go hand in hand. Unfortunately, I'm too low in rank to be involved with the planning or to obtain any information yet on where they might have the prototype. All I know is that the attack is supposed to occur in the next few weeks."

There were still gaps that neither his nor

Hank's report had filled. "So, the CIA had all this info, but you're DEA. Why did you get involved?"

He shifted in his seat, turning to face her. "Do you really have to ask?"

As she met his gaze, the earlier walls he had put up were gone, revealing a depth of unnerving emotion. Insight told her it was personal for him, much as it was for her due to Sylvia's death.

"They killed someone you cared for?" she asked, almost afraid to hear who it was. A wife, girlfriend or partner? She was totally unprepared for him to say, "You."

"Me? I'm here, Alex."

She exploded out of her chair to pace back and forth. He blocked her way and grabbed her arms to still her agitated motion.

"When your dad was killed, they may as well have killed you, too, Di."

She yanked away from his touch. "You think the people behind this—"

"Are members of the drug ring who shot your dad."

She paced again, unwilling to believe that after so long, her father might get justice. Unable to believe that despite the passage of nearly a decade, it continued to matter to Alex.

She faced him. "Why?"

He moved closer, but she took a step back, needing to keep her distance. Her emotions made it too risky to allow herself solace in his arms.

"Why do you think? I want justice. I want closure so we can—"

With an angry slash of her hand, she silenced him. "Don't. I don't need this right now. And I sure don't need you to take up my cause."

"Well, that's a good start at least," he said calmly as he stood in front of her, deceptively still.

"A good start? Why?"

He took the final step that brought him too close for comfort. "Because at least you're finally able to admit your dad's the reason you do what you do. Take the risks you take."

"I don't take risks," she replied, but the statement lacked conviction.

"I've seen your file, *amorcito*."

"But I haven't seen yours."

He held both hands out in front of him, candidly inviting her in. "I'm an open book."

She suspected that he wasn't and she was intrigued by the changes in him. He possessed a confidence and devil-may-care attitude he hadn't a decade earlier. Despite that, or maybe because of it, the briefing had to stop.

"It's late and I have to be up early."

When she turned for the door, he gently grasped her arm. "It's very late. You may want to bunk here."

She looked down at his arm and then followed the muscled line of it up to his face. "That would not be a good idea."

"It's nearly two in the morning. By the time you get downtown…" His voice trailed off since there was no reason for him to finish.

By the time she got home, she would only have a few hours before it would be time to get up. She risked a peek at her watch to confirm the time and then grudgingly agreed. "I'll take the couch."

"Good, 'cause I wasn't offering up the bed." With that, he sauntered back to the table to clean up the remains of their very late dinner.

She grinned at his unexpected swagger and helped him clear the table. After, he walked to the door of what she assumed was the bedroom. "I wish it hadn't happened like this, but I'm not sorry about getting the chance to work with you. See you again." Before she could respond, he muttered, "*Buenas noches.*"

She stood there for quite a while, wondering if it was wiser to stay or to go. She had to trust he would keep it professional. Part of her was thankful for that. The other part…

The other part was clearly wondering how she would deal with him if he didn't.

Chapter 11

Ryder was eager for a respite from the vampire world filled with sex, violence and the quest for power and blood.

The human world could offer so much more sometimes… The joy of seeing Sebastian and Melissa together. Hearing their baby's heartbeat. Partaking of a sunset and a glass of wine while staring at the city below. Making love.

Tonight he wanted those human things. He wanted…

Diana.

And so once again he found himself at her apartment wondering where she could be as the first smell of dawn teased his nostrils and warmed his skin in warning. He was about to leave when he noticed a familiar car and at the wheel—none other than his ex.

Her suit and shirt were wrinkled, as if she had slept in them. In his opinion, a way better condition than one that screamed that she hadn't.

Not that it's any of your business, she responded mentally. She was staring up at him as he balanced on the edge of the fire escape railing.

Snagged, he thought. He slipped off the railing and plummeted to land in front of her with the barest of noise.

"Definitely snagged. What are you doing here?" she asked, an annoyed tone in her words as she placed her hands on her hips. The action pulled open her jacket and revealed her badge, her holster and the dull black grip of her gun. A threatening posture she used with prospective witnesses or suspects.

"Out for a walk." She rolled her eyes and blew out an exasperated sigh.

His vamp sense of smell detected pine with the hint of…man. He stepped closer and brushed back a short lock of hair that had fallen onto her forehead. She shied away nervously.

"A new perfume?" When her discomfort became evident, his gut twisted with jealousy. "I see."

Diana had known he would pick up on things no mortal would, and cursed beneath her breath at his assumption. "It's not like that. Alex—"

"Alex? That was quick."

"Alejandro Garcia. I call him 'Alex.' He's a very old friend, but… Damn it, it's none of your business anyway. You said—"

"I lied." He moved so quickly, she didn't have time to react. He pinned both arms behind her back, bringing her flush against him. With his free hand, he cradled her jaw and rubbed his thumb across her lips. "Tell me you don't want this."

It was impossible to ignore him when every part of her warmed and came to life with his touch. His body was hard, and fit against hers with perfection, like two pieces of a puzzle coming together. The rough pad of his thumb teasing her lips had her blood pounding as she imagined where else he might touch. But she couldn't give in. Was her reaction love, lust or some vampire head game? She had to break free.

"This?" she replied, her words as sharp as his bite. She batted his hand away. "*This* just proves you're more like a man than you think."

"Really? And why is that, darlin'?" He slipped into that smooth Southern drawl that heated her blood and made her imagine sultry nights lying beneath a canopy of Spanish moss.

"Why? Because you're thinking more with your balls than your head." She shoved him away and headed to the door of her building.

Ryder snagged her arm. "Don't do this."

"Don't you understand? Whatever I'm feeling right now, it isn't right. It isn't normal."

He laughed harshly, but didn't release her. Instead he brushed his mouth softly against hers. "What's normal in this world anymore, darlin'?"

"Not this."

"So," he began, his voice low and intimate. "Can Alex give you normal?" He laid his hand on her shoulder and traced the line of her collarbone with his thumb.

"It's not something I've thought about," she lied, ignoring the way his touch ignited her senses and made her body tingle in response. In truth, thoughts of how it had been and could be again with Alex had woken her repeatedly during the course of the night. With sleep beyond reach, she'd left the safe house, hoping distance would grant her peace of mind.

And now this.

Ryder shifted his hand lower until he grazed the upper swell of her breast. Her nipples tightened in response, clearly visible beneath her white shirt. Somehow she kept from moaning as he cupped her and said, "Kids. A house in the suburbs. Nine-to-five like all the masses?"

"Maybe," Diana said huskily, her breath unsteady as he ran his thumb over the stiff peak of her breast. Somehow she kept up her denial. "This isn't what either of us wants. This…uncertainty. This misery."

Ryder withdrew, both physically and emotionally. Standing in front of her, his body tense, his dark gaze searched hers. "Is that all I bring you— misery?"

"I worry where this will lead us."

"There are few options, darlin'. Either being together until death do us part or—"

"Being together forever."

The first hint of the sun broke past the tops of the buildings over lower Manhattan. A melange of reds and oranges sat like a king's mantle on the shoulders of the buildings while the brighter yellow of the sun grew bolder. A beautiful sight. She was hard-pressed to imagine a life where such a sight filled her with dread.

"Diana?" The urgent tone of his voice meant he couldn't linger much longer.

"I'm sorry, Ryder. I know this isn't easy for you, but it's just as hard for me."

"It's not something you need to decide right now, darlin'. It's not—"

She silenced him by slipping the tips of her fingers over his lips. "I know, *amor.* But I also know there's another option."

His face hardened beneath her hand. The other option was that maybe they weren't intended to be together again.

With a curt nod, he stepped away. "You wanted space. So here's me, giving you space."

He leaped upward, landing a story above her on the fire escape. With a second leap and then a third, he disappeared onto the roof of the building and out of sight.

She dropped her head until her chin nearly poked a hole into her chest. Dealing with two ex-lovers in one night was not exactly what she'd planned. She only hoped by the time her investigation into Sylvia's murder and the CDA plot was over, she would have a better idea how to handle her relationships with both men.

She didn't want to consider that there was also the very distinct possibility she wouldn't have to worry about either relationship.

As she unlocked the door to her apartment building it occurred to her that maybe she should think about getting a cat.

Diana introduced herself and her team to the various agents seated around the table, and then she began her report by flashing the first picture onto the screen. The face of a handsome military man filled the space. He was wearing a standard issue U.S. Army uniform, and his chest held a number of medals. "Gonzalo Chavez founded the CDA in 1972 after his return from Vietnam where he earned a Silver Star for gallantry and an honorable discharge.

"After fighting on behalf of the revolution, Chavez was forced to flee Cuba to avoid imprisonment." She glanced at the faces in the darkened room, her gaze settling on Rupert. When he nodded in approval she continued.

"Chavez was recruited by the CIA to join the

ill-fated Bay of Pigs invasion. After his release from a Cuban prison and service in Vietnam, Chavez became very active in Miami politics."

Diana rapidly moved through a series of pictures of Chavez with well-known American politicians until she reach a photo of a young soldier in Desert Storm camouflage.

"Sergeant Antonio Lopez also distinguished himself in combat. He met Chavez in Miami during some protests. The two men hit it off. Within a few months, Lopez had recruited a large number of bodies for the CDA and within two years had expanded the CDA's reach to Union City, New Jersey—once the home of the nation's second-largest Cuban population."

The next slide was of Chavez in fatigues along with Lopez, Moreno and several other young men, all looking strong, healthy and tanned after two weeks of training in the Florida Keys. The CIA had pinpointed these men, all from the New Jersey/New York area, as the most likely to be carrying out the CDA's agenda of an attack on the United Nations or the Cuban Mission.

"Gives new meaning to 'Be All That You Can Be,' doesn't it?" one of the agents in the room quipped, prompting nervous laughter from everyone.

Diana signaled at Rupert to pick up where she'd left off.

"Hank Rupert. CIA," he announced as Diana played a video that highlighted his technical analysis of the stolen hand-held rocket launcher and smart bomb prototype.

"Although we have identified the possible targets, we have yet to determine when the attack is planned, although we expect it will be in the next few weeks," Diana added.

David handed out stacks of papers to each agent. "These are the materials you will need to refresh your understanding of the case and to provide you with the immediate plans for proceeding with a joint investigation."

After Diana delineated the respective roles of each of the agents and answered their questions, the battle plan was clear.

As the agents filed out, ADIC Hernandez walked up to them. "Good job, Reyes. Harris. Rupert. I'll let you know later how the legal eagles have fared with our wiretap requests."

"David and Hank will be staying behind to

finalize any last-minute details this morning. I'll be gone for an hour or so—"

"To see Max Moreno," Jesus interjected.

Diana nodded as she banged some papers on the tabletop to straighten their edges. "Maybe he'll finally be willing to provide some information."

"What about Rodriguez?" Jesus asked.

"The D.A. isn't pressing charges."

"What do you plan to do about de la Fuente's lawyer?" David asked.

"We owe Martinez a visit. I want to make sure he knows he's going down."

Rupert shifted uncomfortably at her words. "Do you think that's wise?"

Her voice was cold as she answered, "I want to break him, Hank." Mainly because she suspected Sylvia's partner had fingered Sylvia for execution.

"It is your case, Special Agent in Charge Reyes. It'll be your ass that gets fried if we fail." Rupert shrugged and walked away.

She stood there with her ADIC and partner, waiting until the CIA agent was long gone before asking, "Why do I feel that he isn't necessarily on our side?"

Chapter 12

Stacia lounged on the ledge of the building, waiting for yet another glimpse of the woman Ryder had visited the other morning. She'd caught only the end of their very passionate display, but it had been enough to compel her interest, not to mention her already growing desire for the handsome vampire.

The scant show had convinced her that beneath Ryder's exterior existed a passion such as she hadn't experienced in many centuries. Not even Diego, one of her favorites, could match it. Especially not now, when despite her taking of him, lordly Diego had been pining for his beloved serving wench Esperanza. The vision they had shared during their interlude—the one of his lover's desiccated remains—had been enough to drain all the enjoyment from the encounter and leave her wanting someone else. Someone who could give her more.

After thousands of years of existence, she craved unique experiences, uncommon lovers, to break the boredom. To fill the loneliness of the interminable days.

Ryder seemed to be just what she needed. On so many levels.

But there was one thing in the way—this human.

A car finally pulled up to the curb. Ryder must have bitten the woman, for her energy sang much like his. Strong. Resolute. Honorable.

She sniffed disdainfully. Honor was decidedly lacking in most of those who yielded to her charms. As for the others, like Diego and his human wannabes, she considered it a treat to suck the last remnants of virtue from them. To make them acknowledge the pleasure to be found in the embrace of the beast.

The woman below—heading now to the entrance of the building—was filled with not only that vile virtue, but with a rich opulent darkness Stacia had never sensed before in a mortal.

Delicious.

She better understood Ryder's fascination now. This woman enriched his power.

Together these two…

Hunger rose up, sharp and demanding as she imagined them joined, making love, imagined feeding from them, fueling herself with their essences, with life, rich with passion and… Could it be love? Real love unlike any she had ever experienced in her undead lifetime?

She needed to know more.

Although the woman would shortly be within reach, Stacia sensed she could not be taken easily.

Ryder on the other hand…

Ryder, beneath the demon, was a man. Throughout the ages, men succumbed all too easily to the charms of a beautiful woman.

A man didn't exist, either alive or undead, who could forego her allure.

With that self-assurance, she went in search of Ryder, certain he would be either at the Lair or the Blood Bank, licking his wounds after the human's rejection. By the time the dawn came, she was sure he would be licking something else.

"Millions of people walking around. Millions of women, waiting to be relished and here we sit," Diego said, slurping down a sip of blood.

Ryder nodded, understanding Diego's frustration. "Stacia and you—"

"She's a witch, that one," Diego mumbled beneath his breath.

"I thought she was a vamp?" he teased his friend, trying to drag him out of his morose mood.

"You do not understand, *mi amigo*. When she takes you… It is like nothing you've ever experienced and yet…" His voice trailed off at the end, uncertain.

"But you went with her."

"Afterward, it is something you never want to experience again. She leaves you…empty."

Ryder laid a hand on the other man's shoulder. "I know it's been hard for you, but there are other vamps out there. Female vamps besides Stacia."

Diego laughed harshly. "Really? Care to join me in this quest, or do you plan on waiting for the human?"

Diana had made it clear she wanted it over between them, no matter how much they cared for one another. Would he ever be able to yank her from his heart? And if not, how long could he wait for her to change her mind?

"Forever is a long time," Diego said.

Humans didn't have forever, Ryder thought. In what might seem like the blink of an eye to a vamp, a human's life came and disappeared. Then others were born and just as quickly dwindled away.

"Have you ever…loved a human?" Ryder asked the older vamp, convinced that he couldn't be alone in caring for a mortal.

"No. *Nunca*. That will bring only pain." Certainty colored Diego's words.

"And Stacia?"

"Ah, Stacia." Diego raised his glass and drained the remaining blood. "Stacia will twist you in knots with wanting her," he said, wrenching his fists back and forth, almost angrily, in emphasis. "You will be on your knees, begging her to take you in. Begging for her bite, and when her teeth sink in…" Diego dropped his hands. "You want her to keep on sucking. To take all of you until nothing remains. Until you are just a big pile of bone and muscle waiting to turn to dust."

When Diego whipped his head around, despair lingered in his gaze. He longed for the vampire he had loved, but also, for an end to his loneliness.

Ryder understood the loneliness well. Before Diana…

THE READER SERVICE™
FREE BOOK OFFER
FREEPOST CN81
CROYDON
CR9 3WZ

NO STAMP
NECESSARY
IF POSTED IN
THE U.K. OR N.I.

He wouldn't think about what it had been like before or what it would be like after she died. Why borrow trouble? Laying a hand on Diego's arm, he said, "It's time to let go. To think about finding someone else."

"And you? Will you let go of her, as well, *amigo?*"

Sorrow came quickly, wrenching his gut and his heart. Despite that, he knew his friend was right. He had to let go.

"Let's get out of here." He stood and surveyed Manhattan from the balcony ledge.

Diego shot an uneasy glance up at him. "Where?"

He thought about the Blood Bank, but Stacia was sure to be there. He wanted a safer venue. "The Lair. We'll find our share of women there on a Saturday night."

Diego snorted, but still he stood and, without a second thought, leaped off the ledge.

Ryder followed.

Being tall, dark and dangerous had definite advantages. Ryder wrapped an arm around the bare midriff of the young woman next to him. She moved easily, her svelte body graceful as she danced. Her dark shoulder-length hair shifted with the movement of her body. Hips swaying against his, she tried to entice his erection to life, but it wasn't happening. Just as it hadn't happened with the three other women he had danced with since arriving at the Lair.

When the song ended, he excused himself and left Diego on the dance floor. He needed wine to wash away the lingering taste of the blood he and Diego had shared earlier. Blood-bag blood. Nothing like…

He refused to dwell upon the sweetness of Diana's blood in his mouth, singing through his veins.

As he approached the bar, he slowed. *Stacia.* He smelled her. The scent of orange blossoms.

They rubbed them into my skin and buried me with them, Stacia said in his mind.

He turned on his heel, looking for her.

Have you missed me?

No.

Her husky chuckle, ripe with promise, echoed through his skull.

Liar. She abruptly stood in front of him,

but not in her vamp getup. Gone was the leather, replaced by a black halter top and sinfully low-rise black jeans. They exposed an enticing amount of skin and toned muscle. A ring of woven gold pierced her navel much like the smaller one threaded through her brow. She could have been any one of the young women crowding the club.

But I'm not anything like them, beloved. She laid a hand on his chest.

Much as he had been during every other encounter, he was fascinated. Especially since, with the leather gone…

She looked so much like Diana. So human.

I can be whatever you like.

As she said that, she opened the first button on his black cotton shirt and then another, enough to part the fabric to midchest. She placed her hand there and it was warm. Mortally warm.

You drained someone? He covered her hand with his. Her skin was soft and his touch roused the fragrance of flowers once more. But beneath that scent… He inhaled deeply. The aroma of her was intoxicating, musky femininity flush with need.

She closed the distance between them. "No draining, my love. I know how much you hate that thought. Just a little nip, here and there. Like a hummingbird sampling nectar."

Her breath bathed his cheek. Mortally warm and with the clean scent of mint, not blood. When her lips slipped over the line of his jaw, to his ear, he placed his hand at her waist. Her skin was smooth, absent the chill of the undead. Her muscles toned and hard.

"You like this, don't you?" she whispered. "You like that I look like her. That I'm warm like her."

"You can't ever be her," he said, but despite that, he groaned as she eased her hand beneath his shirt and traced the edge of his nipple.

No, love, I can't ever be her. But you can't ever have her again, can you? She brought her hips to caress his, dragging another unwilling moan from him.

"Dance with me," she commanded softly, her lips hovering over his mouth.

Just a dance, he thought, not wanting to anger her. She had too much power to risk that.

You can have that power, as well. You can feel

that power in your hands. Surrounding you. Suck that power within you.

As if to prove her point, a wave of energy built around them and with a slight motion of her hand, it crashed over him, filling him with so much sensation his head spun and every inch of his body flared to life. It was like being drunk on some intoxicating liquor, everything alive and yet woozy, every part of his body craving more.

"Stacia." He wrapped his arms around her waist, needing stability. It brought his aroused body against hers and she moaned, equally caught up in the explosion of energy she had released.

"That's just the start, beloved. Imagine it." She moved the hand trapped between their bodies downward until she stroked him slowly through his jeans. When she whispered into his ear, her voice was needy, on the edge of pain. "Imagine my warmth, Ryder. Like her, only forever."

Ryder gulped in a breath and she filled his senses again. The orange blossoms, so heady. The musk of her arousal, so…human. Her dark hair brushed against his face. Silky. Soft.

When she shifted her mouth and put her lips

to his, her fresh breath spilled against him, was alive in his mouth as her tongue darted in.

She moaned with a human need long unsatisfied. "Ryder, please."

God help him, he was fighting a losing battle to ignore her plea.

Chapter 13

Diana couldn't say no. It was part of her job to get whatever information she could for her team. Even if that meant meeting Alex in the safe house—a place that wasn't necessarily so safe for her.

She couldn't explain why she felt the way she did. It wasn't a secret tryst or anything. So why had Alex stayed on her mind in a much too personal way since the other night?

Maybe because it had felt so normal, the voice of reason interjected.

It had felt right, she reluctantly admitted. Right in a way she could never have with Ryder. Another reason why she needed to forget Ryder and to get on with her life—a life not filled with the undead.

Being with Alex—it had almost been like

before her father's death and darkness had gripped her life, before she had left Alex and let her world spiral out of control.

A part of her reasoned that if Alex truly cared, she wouldn't have been able to push him away quite so easily. But as memories filled her of just how many times he had tried to break past the walls she had erected, it occurred to her that it hadn't been easy for him. He had battled hard for her, but lost.

She had expected it might be difficult to see him again after so many years. And yet once they'd gotten past that initial discomfort, it had been relatively painless to slip into the patterns of old. Maybe too painless. But it also felt different in a way that piqued her curiosity. Different because Alex was definitely not the same man he had been nearly a decade ago.

In the past few days she had spent too much time thinking about him during those very rare moments when she wasn't concentrating on a case that was going nowhere. For every move they made, the CDA seemed to be one move ahead. Moreno hadn't cracked. De la Fuente wasn't talking. Martinez hadn't broken a sweat when she'd visited him.

Luckily, Alex thought he had a lead and so here she was, waiting for him to arrive. Her stomach grumbled and she hoped Alex would think to bring dinner. He always seemed to know just how to satisfy…

She stopped herself right there. Instead, she set the table in anticipation of a meal. If Alex hadn't thought to bring food…

He opened the door and stepped inside, a bag in his hand from another of the Cuban restaurants along Bergenline.

She smiled. "You read my mind."

A dark, dangerous look crept onto his face. When he spoke, the tones of his voice were bedroom-low. "Can you read mine?"

Dios mio, but he couldn't possibly be thinking that, she worried and bit her lower lip. Heat flared within her at the recollection of what that look used to mean.

A moment later, however, he grinned, his teeth white against his tanned skin, his green eyes sparkling with merriment.

"Gotcha. Actually, I was thinking of how cute it is to see you being all domestic," he said as he sauntered over in another pair of wickedly tight jeans and placed the bag in the center of the table.

She playfully poked the hard muscle of his midsection with a fork. "Not fair, Alexito."

Grinning again, he snatched the utensil from her fingers. "Alexito. No one else has ever called me that."

Wanting to get even for his earlier little prank, she teased in a falsetto, "'Oh, Alexito. Please, Alexito. A little more, *Papi.*'"

He shifted closer and brought his hand to her waist, inched his mouth near to her ear to whisper, "Not since you, *amorcito*. The rest wouldn't dare."

Even through the cotton of her shirt the heat of his hand enticed her. The slight roughness of his palm when it snagged the fabric made her think of his hand brushing over other places—sensitive places—as he busied himself with removing the takeout from the bag.

Danger, Diana. She was obviously confused and on the rebound. That was the reason for all these erotic thoughts.

"So what have you heard?" she asked, trying to force the discussion back to business.

Alex glanced at her shrewdly, obviously aware of her ploy. She also knew that for the moment, he was content to play her game. But only for the moment. That was also clear.

"Heard a rumor that Lopez loaned the weapon to the Colombians."

"With the attack supposedly weeks away?" She joined Alex in opening up the assorted aluminum plates holding the food. No choices tonight, she realized. Just roast pork, rice and black beans with the obligatory sides of both ripe and green plantains. The aroma from the pork was heavenly, a mix of citrus, garlic and cumin. The beans had an earthier scent, but just as delicious.

"Lopez isn't stupid. He's got to have a reason why he would give up the weapon. A very good reason."

"Which we don't know," she reminded him.

He paused with a forkful of rice and beans halfway to his mouth. "No, we don't. What I do know is that someone is headed to Corona tomorrow to pick it up."

"Well, that's a start. Do you know where?" While Corona wasn't very large, it might be difficult to track Lopez along the tight city streets.

"Don't know where. That'll be up to your team to find out. The CDA members have been in plain sight up until now. Follow them—"

"And we'll find the weapon." She ate a piece of the succulent pork, considering his report. Considering him as he sat across from her.

He looked up. "What?"

"You couldn't have found a secure line and relayed that information without a face-to-face?"

Alex mixed together some rice and beans, forked up a good amount, but paused with the utensil halfway to his mouth. "I didn't feel like eating dinner alone. How about you?"

She didn't know if she could call grabbing a sandwich at her desk dinner.

"I didn't feel like it, either," she confessed.

The conversation turned to slightly more personal things, although not anything too personal. She was grateful that Alex recognized the limits she had silently set.

Dinner was close to complete when her cell phone chimed with the ringtone that identified her brother. As she opened the phone, the face urgently flashed the time. Nearly midnight...

"Sebastian! Is she having the baby?"

"We just got to the hospital, but you need to hurry. Melissa seems to be in a rush."

Sebastian was about to have a baby, but instead of happy images, visions of Sylvia lying dead with her child rushed to the forefront of Diana's mind.

"Diana?"

"Go be with Melissa. I'll be there…soon," she replied, but could hear the hesitation in her own voice.

"You are coming, right?"

She forced a tight smile. "I'll be there soon, *hermanito*. I promise." She flipped her phone closed.

"Something up?"

"Sebastian's having a baby," she answered, unnerved by the emotions the call had roused almost as much as the realization that her brother was going to be a father. She had always imagined she'd be the first parent, being the oldest. As Alex squeezed her hand in reassurance, she thought about how often she had once imagined him as the father.

"I assume it's Sebastian's wife who's having the baby," Alex quipped, trying to draw her out of her unusual mood.

She chuckled as he intended and tugged on his hand in mock punishment. "Yes, Sebastian's wife."

"Do you like her?" he asked, twining his fingers with hers to keep the connection she had allowed in her moment of distress.

"Melissa's the best. She's made Sebastian very happy. Why do you ask?"

His broad shoulders rose and fell in a hesitant shrug. "I just noticed something there. Words you weren't saying."

Disturbed by his observation, she jerked her hand from his and stalked a few steps away from the table before she faced him again. Suddenly some of those words she hadn't said spewed from her. "I worry about him and what he's gotten himself into," she said, although she couldn't say that it was because Sebastian had married a vampire's keeper. Or that Sebastian's child would be next in line for the dubious honor of that position.

"You and your dad always worried about Sebastian, but he's a strong man with a good heart."

Funny that he had seen that so long ago when she hadn't.

"There's more, isn't there, *amor?*" Alex cradled her cheek. His palm, rough against her skin, unintentionally roused those earlier unwanted thoughts.

"I…" She stopped, unsure of just what to say. "I saw Sylvia… When Sebastian first called, I saw her. Dead. With her dead baby."

He wrapped his arms around her. Comfort flooded her. Comfort and a sense of security she hadn't felt in a long time. She slipped her hands to his back, tentative at first, but then gripped him harder, accepting the solace he offered.

"I'm sorry. I can't imagine how difficult this must be."

She said nothing. She couldn't or she'd risk unleashing tears. Instead she screwed her eyes shut and buried her head against his chest, taking deep breaths until she regained balance. As she did so, he rubbed his hands up and down her back in a soothing gesture.

Finally she skirted back a bit. "I'm okay now. I have to go."

"Do you want…company?" he questioned uncertainly, as if afraid she would push him away.

"Can you risk it?" She hadn't worried about

meeting him at the safe house since it was
supposed to be, well, safe. But out in public,
someone might see them together. If they realized
that she was FBI…

He cupped her face in his hands, his touch
tender. "No one is keeping an eye on me. After
all, I'm just a lowly foot soldier. But just in case,
tell me where to meet you."

Meeting his gaze, she knew he would keep his
promise and, surprisingly, she needed him there.
She didn't know why, except that she was unprepared to meet the latest addition to the Reyes
family alone. She blurted out the hospital's address.

He smiled and dropped a quick kiss on her
lips. "I'll be there."

With that, he motioned to the table piled with
their dirty dishes, grinned and said, "Sorry to
force you to be domestic again."

"Now wait a second—" she began but didn't
get to finish as he strode out the door.

She glared at the table. As she cleaned and
provided Alex the time needed to put some distance between them, she considered how to read
that man the riot act about what he could and

could not expect her to do. Dishes being high on the list of did-not-dos.

She just wasn't good at domestic.

By the time she finished making the list of all those did-not-dos, however, she was smiling.

Chapter 14

His head pounded with the fury of a thousand drums beating at once. He grabbed it tightly, moaned and sat up. As he did so, the crisp sheets of his bed rubbed naked skin. The last thing he remembered was being in the club with…

"Stacia."

"I'm right here, beloved." She dragged his attention to the far corner of the room where she sat fully clothed, a glass of blood dangling loosely in her hand.

Shit. What had happened? He couldn't remember a thing beyond being on the dance floor, bathing in her sexual energy as he stood within her arms.

"Nothing," came her too quick reply.

"Nothing?" he repeated since his body felt as

if it had been pummeled and his dick… He almost reached down to make sure he still had it.

"Nothing." She placed the glass on a nearby table and rose. She walked toward him, her hips swaying enticingly, and images buffeted his mind of those hips moving on him. Riding him to a climax.

"Wishful thinking," she teased.

Do you know everything I'm thinking?

Everything. She sat on the edge of the bed and ran her thumb over his nipple. The movement created a need so strong, an erection immediately sprang to life between his legs.

"Mercy, darlin'," he said and fell back on the bed, breathing raggedly.

"Call out all you want, Ryder. Plead to be free of this." Stacia bent and licked his nipple.

"Why?" he asked on a groan.

"Because I can, beloved, only…"

She stopped then, withdrawing from him completely, taking with her the passion that had enslaved him just a second before.

Breathing erratically, his heart thrumming against his ribs, Ryder rose up on his elbows. "Why did you stop?"

Stacia smiled slyly and returned to her position

across the room. "Because I can, which is why nothing happened tonight."

She didn't want to tell him that her reasons for stopping now had more to do with her suspicion that his honor would rise to the forefront again, bringing guilt. She did not want to deal with any more guilt tonight. Not when she was feeling almost…satisfied from their lovemaking of the past few hours. And quite replete with the blood in her glass—his blood. She'd tasted him both during and after. He was deliciously full-bodied with all those human emotions still alive within him.

Not that she had let him totally release those emotions this night. From the moment in the bar when she had unleashed her vamp power on him, she had known he couldn't resist her. Surprisingly, taking him that way—with his will subjugated—had been unfulfilling. Especially when thoughts of *her*—of the human—swirled in his head.

The annoying ringing of the phone shattered the moment. It had interrupted them before, while she had been in the midst of taking him. With a flick of her hand, she said, "Silence that."

The sharpness of her tone surprised Ryder, but he picked it up. Sebastian's voice came across the line. "We've been trying to reach you."

Concern for his keeper drove away any other emotion Ryder was experiencing, including the disquiet that Stacia wasn't being truthful about the events of the night. "Is Melissa okay?"

"Melissa and the baby are doing fine. They'll be bringing them up to the room soon."

"What did she have?" he asked, wondering what color flowers to bring, which just earned an annoyed sigh from the vamp across the room.

"A girl. A beautiful girl," Sebastian said, his voice brimming with a father's pride.

"I'll be there in a bit. Is Diana... Is she there?"

"Not yet, but I expect her soon."

If Ryder was going to keep things right between all of them, he had to be able to handle seeing her. "I'll be there shortly."

"Running to her so soon like a good little pet?" Stacia asked, her tone filled with scorn.

"Better to run to someone than away, don't you think?" he parried, sensing she was hiding something beneath her surface.

He knew he had struck home when she said,

"Don't presume to know anything about me, Ryder."

Rising, he grabbed at his clothes, which were strewn across the floor of his bedroom. "I know nothing about you because you won't let me."

She slammed her glass down then exploded in a burst of vamp speed to stand in front of him. "Do you know what it's like to be me? To have lived as long as I have with…" She closed her eyes and inclined her head away from him, as if afraid she revealed too much. He perceived her pain then, raw and infinitely alive. Like she was. Eternally in pain.

"Eventually, you'll let someone know. Maybe then, you won't be so alone."

He didn't wait for her reply or linger to offer any other solace. Instead, thoughts of seeing the new baby and Diana rushed him out the door.

By the time Diana met Alex in the lobby of the hospital and they made it to the maternity ward, the newest Reyes was already with her mother and father. Melissa had the baby cradled to her breasts, a pale pink blanket swaddled around the child. Sebastian hovered nearby, peering at the newborn with unabashed glee.

When her brother noticed her, he gave her a broad smile that turned to one of surprise when he saw her companion.

"Alex. Long time no see."

She hugged her brother while Alex nodded at Melissa in greeting. "Alejandro Garcia. I'm an old family friend."

Melissa, tired but happy, smiled and looked at Diana. "We named her Mariel Elizabeth Reyes after the grandmas. Would you like to hold her?"

Hold her?

"Come on, big brave FBI agent sister. Mariel won't break."

Hands shaky, she accepted the tiny bundle. "Make sure to support her head," Melissa said.

The baby had caramel-colored hair, a definite mix of her mother's and father's colors. Her small cupid's bow lips puckered and opened as miniature fists boxed the air. Beneath the blanket, her legs squirmed, but quieted as Diana softly sang the opening verses of a lullaby. *"Arruru mi niña, arruru mi amor."*

At the sound of her low melodic voice, the baby's eyes opened, surprisingly alert and a deep blue. "She's beautiful," Diana said, awe in her voice.

Alex laid one hand on her shoulder. "So beautiful. Like her mother and aunt."

Weirdness settled in her gut. The strangeness of holding Mariel. Of having Alex beside her. Long ago, she had envisioned sharing such a moment with him, only the child had been theirs. She pushed that thought away, as she did thoughts of never holding Ryder's child or sharing that joy with him.

Eventually, Mariel complained in earnest, her legs kicking fitfully beneath the swaddling blanket.

"I think it's feeding time, Mom." She passed the baby back to Melissa. "Let's go, Alex."

At his puzzled look, she said, "Feeding time as in private time."

Outside in the hall, she faced him, both happy and unsure. "It's hard to believe, isn't it?"

"It is." He rocked back and forth on his heels, also clearly conflicted. "You looked beautiful holding that baby."

Confession time, she thought. "It felt awkward at first, but right. Must be that clock ticking inside of me. Thirty will do that to a woman."

He brought his thumb to her lips, sending a blast of heat through her.

"It felt weird for me, too. Seeing you like that, but the child not being mine."

"Alex—"

He didn't give her the chance to protest, replacing his finger with his mouth. Kissing her until her head was spinning and she had to grab his shoulders for stability.

"Alex, this is crazy. Especially now," she said, and yet she couldn't keep herself from going on tiptoe and kissing him back.

He wrapped his arms around her and dragged her tight to him. "Don't push me away again."

His words shattered the moment and she did just that. They were both breathing roughly as they squared off. "I'm sorry, Alex."

"Don't be sorry. Just be sure of what you want. There won't be a third time for us." He turned on his heel and stalked away.

She watched his retreating back much as she had ten years earlier. Only this time…

She couldn't just stand there and let him walk out of her life. Not when he might be the one man who could help her forget a certain vampire. "Alex!"

He turned, a look of surprise on his face.

"Wait up!"

Chapter 15

An errant thorn from one of the pink roses sank deep into Ryder's palm when Diana kissed the man.

A handsome Latino. Tall and strong-bodied. Clearly enamored of her. Human.

Anger reared up in him, bringing an unwanted rush of heat. The vampire broke free, eager for blood. Ryder's breathing was harsh and his body trembled with the savagery he subdued. He focused on the pain of the thorn in his palm to bring humanity back.

A regular guy. Just what Diana needed, he told himself. As difficult as it was to behold their emotionally charged exchange, honor demanded he keep his distance and give her the space she had requested. Especially now, when Diana had discovered something that could give her the kind of life she wanted. The kind of life she deserved.

A life unlike the one he could give her.

Taking a deep breath to drive away any lingering traces of the vampire, he walked to the door of Melissa's room.

When Sebastian opened the door he shot an uneasy look up and down the hall.

"She's gone. Left with her…friend." The memory brought a rush of angry heat and Ryder took a deep breath to keep the vampire at bay as he stepped into the room.

Melissa sat in bed, rearranging the front of her shirt. The faint smell of sweet mother's milk teased his lingering vamp senses.

He sat on the edge of the bed. "Are you okay?" he questioned, fatherly concern coloring his voice.

"A little sore, but otherwise fine." She held out the bundle of pink to him.

He juggled the roses until Sebastian took them and walked out under the guise of finding a vase.

Ryder took Melissa's hand. "Are you sure you're okay?"

Melissa smiled tiredly. "I'm fine. This is a typical thing, you know."

He wanted to say that he did, only it had been

a long time since he'd been in this position. "The last baby I held was you."

"Well, then. It's time you held the next Danvers baby, isn't it?" She thrust the baby out to him again, leaving him no choice. Carefully cradling the baby's head, he nestled her to his chest and examined the newest Danvers. No, make that Reyes.

"She's beautiful."

"I think so, but I'm prejudiced, Uncle Ryder."

He smiled and repeated, "Uncle Ryder. I like the sound of that." It occurred to him that this was as good a time as any to tell her. "I want to keep it to just that."

Melissa's eyebrows scrunched together in confusion. "Huh? What do you—"

"You're the *last* Danvers. This Reyes baby won't be burdened with the responsibility of being my keeper. I don't need one now—"

"That you've got Diana and a crew of undead friends?"

"Let's leave it at, I've got friends."

Too smart to miss anything, Melissa said, "You saw her with Alex?"

He shrugged noncommittally. "I did. Out in the hallway. They seemed…well-suited."

"Sebastian says they dated back in college. That they were serious." The baby began to squirm and she held her hands out for the child. "She's a pig." Melissa brought the baby to her breast.

As he watched Melissa and her baby, he imagined how one day Diana might also have a child. Watch it grow. Become a grandmother if…

He gave her a chance with someone else. Someone human.

"She should be able to experience this," he said morosely.

"She's the one to make that decision, Ryder. Not you."

"Meaning?"

"Meaning that if she comes back, she's made that choice."

Melissa obviously knew him well enough to know that he might second-guess Diana's decision if she returned. And if she didn't?

He met Melissa's gaze and realized she recognized his dilemma. Understood the pain that would come regardless of whether he lost Diana now or lost her later.

"We'll deal with whatever happens, Uncle Ryder."

With a nod, he rose just as Sebastian returned. "Going already?"

"I've got things to do." He departed with a surge of vamp speed before Sebastian could utter a word.

Diana faced a busy morning with lots of assignments. Some were already in place, like the extra surveillance on Lopez. In less than half an hour, she would hold a special meeting of the joint teams and hand over the search warrants they had obtained, courtesy of the information provided by Alex.

Her Alex, she thought, and sighed as she remembered the tender kisses they had shared, thought about the way he had looked at her as she'd held Sebastian's new baby. It was almost too easy to imagine how it might have been if Fate hadn't tossed them from their chosen path with the death of her father.

Wishful thinking, or thoughts provoked because she was on the rebound?

Even with Alex's presence, she still missed Ryder, forced him from her thoughts more than she cared to admit. She even occasionally wondered what was up with his vampire friends who had turned out to be fairly likable once you got past that whole "creature of the night" thing.

When her mind wandered before sleep, the lack of Ryder's big body next to her brought emptiness to her heart and longing for the way he understood her needs. He was strong enough to deal with the more complicated and severe facets of her soul.

But she had little time to daydream further. David walked into the conference room where she had been waiting for the team to assemble.

"Peter and Hank are here."

She rose and greeted the two men and was about to get started on the briefing when ADIC Hernandez walked in, a broad smile on his face.

"Good news. Moreno's lawyer just called. Moreno wants to talk."

"Just like that?" Peter asked.

Her ADIC confirmed it with a nod and said, "Reyes was right that he would eventually break."

"Seems convenient that he would do it now, doesn't it? Right when we're prepared to nail one of them as they pick up the device," she said.

"You think Lopez planned this to delay us?" Hank asked, censure dripping from every word.

"I think we should go on this morning as scheduled."

Her words earned an annoyed snort from the older agent. "You're seeing ghosts everywhere, Reyes."

"We will continue with our surveillance of Lopez and the others," ADIC Hernandez said, stopping any further discussion. "Agent Harris. Detective Daly. I'm trusting you to get the task started while the rest of us go see Moreno."

Hank pursed his lips and wagged his head in disbelief. "It's your call, Hernandez."

She rose from the table and leaned toward Hank. "No, Hank. It's *my* call. You seem to forget that."

"Like I said before—"

"It's my ass on the line if we fail. I heard you the first time." Straightening, she grabbed the search warrants and passed them to David and Peter before they left the room.

Hank rose. "I need a moment before we go," he said, and exited without getting her approval.

She met her ADIC's worried gaze. "He's trouble, Jesus. I feel it in my gut."

"Let's hope you're wrong, Diana. Ready to go see Moreno?"

When she nodded, they went in search of Rupert, who stood outside the door, as if waiting for them. At their appearance, however, he did an abrupt about-face and walked away. Presumably toward the interrogation room.

Diana arched an eyebrow as she mumbled, "Definitely trouble."

Chapter 16

Max Moreno gave up the names of Steve Martinez and various CDA members in exchange for immunity. Based on his testimony and the information Alex had provided, they now knew where the weapon would be and who would be picking it up. None other than Antonio Lopez himself.

Diana glanced across the street, her gaze focused on Lopez despite the stream of traffic on Queens Boulevard. He entered a one-story, cinder-block building nestled beneath the Seven subway line. The sign on the side of the building indicated it was a metalwork shop.

She radio'd the N.Y.P.D. and FBI agents surrounding the building. "Lopez is in. Keep an eye on all exits. Do not move until we advise."

David waited across the street near the mouth

of a narrow alley. Rupert stood beside her, his stance anxious as they awaited Lopez's exit. It took close to fifteen minutes before their target emerged with a long, rectangular cardboard box.

Diana asked Rupert, "Do the dimensions of that box seem right for the device?"

"Yes. Let's move in."

"All units, secure the target and location." Diana raced across the street, dodging traffic. Rupert plodded behind her, his steps heavier and slower.

By the time she arrived at the building, David had Lopez stomach-down on the sidewalk, his hands and legs spread-eagled. David kept his gun trained on the man and a knee in the middle of his back. The cardboard box lay a few feet away at Peter's feet.

"Antonio Lopez?" she asked.

The man looked up at her from his awkward position. "And you would be?" he said with not a whit of concern as David patted him down for weapons.

She flashed her badge and was about to answer when she heard over her earpiece, "All's secure inside."

"Do not let anyone move," she instructed her

team. Returning her attention to Lopez, she said, "Special Agent in Charge Reyes, Mr. Lopez."

"What's the reason for this unauthorized detention?" Lopez said as David yanked him to his feet and slapped the warrant on Lopez's chest.

"Antonio Lopez. We have a warrant for—"

Lopez silenced her with a wave of the warrant in his hand. "I can read, *niña*. So search away."

Cocky, she thought. How she wished she had Lopez somewhere else with some of her vamp friends. That cockiness would last all of a second. But she wasn't in some back alley and Lopez clearly thought he had the upper hand. Which meant he was either totally stupid or smart enough to have realized he was being watched or…

She didn't want to consider the last possibility—that someone had tipped him off.

Rupert approached with the box and she motioned for him to open it. He did. It contained nothing other than chrome custom-worked pipes and other smaller metal pieces.

"Well?" she asked, hoping that once assembled it would—

"It's not what we want," Hank said.

She met Lopez's smug and decidedly pleased look. Motioning to Peter, who stood off to the side with the SWAT officers, she said, "Can you search the van with Agent Rupert? David and I are heading inside the shop." Over the earpiece, Diana instructed the two FBI agents to secure the back exits of the shop.

The building was much like one would expect inside. An assortment of pipes, sheet metal and other supplies lined one wall while lathes, punch presses and other metal-working machines took up the greater part of the space.

About a dozen or more individuals stood, hands tucked behind their heads as the two FBI agents, accompanied by a duo of SWAT officers, manned each corner of the room, weapons at the ready. The shop workers were edgy, some more than others. Most likely because they were undocumented aliens.

She called out, *"No somos La Migra. Necessitamos informacíon sobre Antonio Lopez."*

At the news that they weren't Immigration, a number of the workers relaxed, but not all. She continued onward, seeing nothing of interest until reaching the back of the building. The surfaces of the tables there held sundry parts, pipes, nuts and bolts. Three men waited anxiously, close to the exit.

This trio was different. Better dressed. Not as tired-looking. She approached one and asked him to show his hands. When he pretended he didn't understand, she repeated her instructions in Spanish.

He lowered his hands and displayed the tops and then his palms.

Just what she expected—nothing. "Put them back up. Now!"

David peered at the table's surface. "Di. Come take a look."

She noticed it then. A footprint smack in the middle of the clutter. A short distance away, another one. She looked up at the drop ceiling.

"Does that one seem out of—"

She didn't get to finish as the three men rushed the door. One man grabbed the FBI agent's weapon, but not before David and she had drawn their guns. He didn't get a chance to fire as they dropped him with a volley of shots, but the other two men escaped out the back door. "All units. Two suspects on the loose."

A blast of gunfire meant the units were already responding. She and David raced to the door, where an injured SWAT officer motioned in the direction of another alley. "That way. They're armed. Semi-automatics."

David sprinted ahead of her.

She cursed the riskiness of his haste, but chased after him. As they reached one corner where the alley branched out, gunfire erupted.

"I got one," she heard in her earpiece. As they rounded the corner one of the CIA agents stood over the suspect. A blossoming stain of blood marred the middle of the man's chest as he lay flat on his back, his eyes wide open and glazed.

"Shit," she said, and met David's gaze. "We need them alive, damn it."

He nodded and hurried down the alley in the other direction with her on his tail. The alley opened onto one of Corona's busier streets. Mom-and-Pop-size stores lined both sides and people darted here and there at the sound of gunfire. All except one man about half a block ahead, who moved a little too slowly considering all the ruckus.

Diana laid her hand on David's arm and

motioned for him to follow her. She kept her distance for a number of reasons. First, she didn't want a gun battle with so many civilians around. Second, the suspect might lead them to others.

As he crossed the street to a block with less activity, he realized he'd been spotted. Whirling, he drew his weapon and opened fire. Diana only had a moment to think. The first round made a loud thunk as it slammed into her body armor. She fired at his knee to drop him, but he kept on shooting.

The blow to her shoulder had stunned her momentarily, as did the loud explosion of David's gun. A clean hit to the suspect's shoulder. He still didn't go down, which left her no choice.

She aimed and fired. Dead center of his forehead.

David placed a hand on her arm as she continued to train her weapon on the suspect's body. "You okay?"

Her left shoulder and upper arm were numb. The slug the vest had stopped glinted brightly against the dark blue of her windbreaker. Looking at David, she noted a hole in his lower right side. "Are you?"

"For now. I know I'm going to be as sore as shit later."

As she approached the suspect, she told the rest of the team, "Third suspect is down at the corner of…" She noted the location and called it out. She looked at her partner. "Will you stay here while I go back to the van?"

He nodded and she slowly walked back to the primary location, hoping that by the time she got there, she'd have use of her left arm again. At the corner, Hank Rupert waited for her, a pleased smile on his face. One she suspected had nothing to do with the mission and everything to do with her discomfort.

"Have a little problem, Special Agent in Charge Reyes?"

"Fuck you, Hank." She brushed past him, which only brought a painful twinge to the arm where pins and needles signaled the return of sensation.

Peter Daly stood by Lopez's van while Lopez himself leaned against it, his hands cuffed behind him. Lopez grinned when he saw her, but said nothing.

Peter, however, rushed forward. "Are you—"

"I'm fine, but I'll need a few men to help me finish the search inside."

He motioned for some of his uniformed officers to help her.

"Thanks," she said. As both she and Peter's gazes shifted to Lopez, Peter asked, "What do you want me to do with him?"

What she wanted to do was wrong. She wanted Peter to kick the shit out of him until they had the information they needed. That would have been the vampire way. Efficient. Remorseless. Only she wasn't a vamp even though they had influenced her life too much lately. Mortal rules still had to be followed. "We're taking him into custody."

In the shop, her team tore the place apart and discovered something they hadn't expected— parts and semi-assembled launchers hidden in the drop ceiling. Right above where David had noticed the footprints.

As they bagged the parts as evidence, Hank finally strolled in. "Not good. They were making copies."

Copies of a weapon that was still missing.

She cursed beneath her breath and clutched her shoulder as pain blossomed fully.

"You okay?" Peter asked. "You look kinda pale."

A chill marked her skin and nausea roiled her stomach, a delayed reaction to the trauma of the bullet's impact. She battled it back. There was still too much left to do. "I'm okay. Will you take Lopez in for me?"

"Sure." He motioned to her shoulder. "You going to do something about that?"

She gingerly removed her FBI windbreaker and vest. "Later. Right now, we need to go talk to Moreno and Martinez again."

Chapter 17

Moreno and Martinez, however, were dead. Moreno of an apparent heart attack and Martinez from a self-inflicted gunshot wound.

After a quick briefing with all the staff involved in the investigation, it became obvious that the suspects at the various locations they had planned to search had not only been prepared for the FBI's visits, but they refused to talk about anything. By tomorrow, news of Moreno's and Martinez's deaths would make them totally uncooperative. Worse, the authorities could only hold Lopez for twenty-four hours without charging him and they had nothing on him.

She had no idea who she could trust outside of her closest circle of colleagues.

Hank Rupert seemed a little too smug about the

setbacks. Given their hostility toward one another, that was not unexpected. But could he be a mole? Tough to contemplate, much less prove.

When she called it a night, she motioned for Hank to stay with her, David and ADIC Hernandez. He did so grudgingly, which only served to pique her interest.

"What's the matter, Hank? Keeping you from a hot date?" she questioned with some bite, trying to goad the man in the hope he might reveal something. Anything.

"Old bones aren't what they used to be." He stretched to emphasize the point.

She didn't believe him. Was he eager to leave so he could meet someone? Maybe whoever had been behind the two murders that day? If there was one thing she was certain of, it was that Moreno and Martinez had been executed.

"Moreno's heart attack is kind of suspicious, but nothing's come up in the autopsy to indicate foul play," she said.

Rupert shrugged. "People die of heart attacks all the time."

"Seems to me you would know about that. Making it seem like a heart attack," David said, surprising her. Although she had mentioned how uneasy she was about the two incidents, she hadn't told David about her belief that someone had leaked information. What David proposed now went well beyond a leak. Amazingly, she didn't think him wrong.

When Rupert didn't answer, she asked, "Is it possible Moreno was poisoned and we won't be able to determine it?"

Hank's words were clipped and laced with anger. "You think I had something to do with this?"

"The CDA knew about the raids and someone made it clear what would happen to those who talked by disposing of Moreno and Martinez," Jesus Hernandez interjected. "Any idea which CDA member might want to do that, Hank?"

Hank hunched his thickly muscled shoulders with an indifference that didn't match the irritation apparent on his face. "Lopez is a soldier. He's sure to have a chain of command in place and that person—"

"Who would that person be?" Diana asked.

"Why don't you ask lover boy?" Hank taunted, and Diana got right in his face.

"Hank, let me make it clear. Stay out of my personal life. As for Garcia, he's *your* operative and, yes, I will ask him since that's part of *my* job."

"Those late-night meetings must be an interesting part of your job, Special Agent in Charge," Hank replied.

"Get out of here, Hank. Before I forget you're a colleague."

Hank chuckled and left the three staring after his swaying bowlegged stride. When she faced David and her ADIC, she noted the concerned expressions on both their faces.

Jesus spoke first. "Diana, we need to be careful around him."

"I don't trust the old bastard," David added.

"I agree. In the meantime, I'm going to meet with Garcia. See what he has to say about the chain of command and who may have given the instructions for these executions."

David shifted his gaze to look at his feet, obviously uncomfortable.

"David. Is there something else you want to say?"

He met her gaze squarely and pulled his shoul-

ders back. "How do you know you can trust
Garcia?"

"I don't."

Chapter 18

Alex was already waiting for her in the apartment when she arrived, the table set with yet more Cuban food. The aroma was heavenly and her stomach responded with a noisy growl.

"Hungry, *amorcito?*" he asked with a carefree smile as he approached her.

She snapped up her hand like a policeman directing traffic.

Alex stopped dead in his tracks. The expression on his face went from "Damn glad you're here" to totally confused.

"What the hell's up with you?"

What was up with her? Annoyance. Anger. The fear of betrayal. Had the food and solace, the "good ol' times we had" ploy just been intended to distract her?

"The more important question is, 'What's going

on, Alex?' What's with the food, and us?" she asked.

"You have to ask that? You have to wonder why I'd want things to be like they used to be?"

In a second that seemed to spin out for an eternity, she realized that what she had felt for him at nineteen wasn't the same emotion she was now experiencing.

"Things can never be like they were before. Never." She paced back and forth before whirling to face him. "Do you know what happened in Corona? With Martinez and Moreno?"

His face went white. He shook his head. "I got a call from one of the unit leaders, warning me about talking to anyone. I never suspected…" He looked down at his feet, his head still shaking in disbelief before he snapped it back up to nail her with his gaze. "They're dead, aren't they?"

She stood in front of him, silent, arms wrapped around herself. When he reached for her, she shrugged off his hand, aggravating the sore spot near her shoulder.

"What happened?"

"Got shot. Vest stopped the bullet."

"Got shot? Just like that?" She had no chance

to react as he grabbed her arms and shook her. "What were you thinking? Don't you realize that…" Words failed him. He relaxed his hold and drew her into his arms. "*Dios,* I'm sorry. It's just… I don't want to lose you again."

She was tense in his embrace, but as the sincerity of his emotion seeped through her defensive shell she relaxed. There was no doubting his reaction. She regretted ever having doubted him.

Laying her head on his chest, she slipped her arms around him and held on tight. "I'm sorry, Alex. I just don't know what to think anymore."

"Don't you? I've never stopped loving you."

His words brought tears to her eyes and pain deep within. She closed her eyes against the intensity of his gaze, afraid of what would happen next. "You don't know what loving me means."

He gently brushed his lips against her forehead. "I know it won't be easy, but I want you in my life. I want to try to have…" He wrapped his arms around her more tightly.

She finally dragged forth the strength to look up at him. His face was so familiar and yet so different. Placing her hand on his jaw, she traced the strong line of it, leaner now with age, more masculine, but still an adoring boy beneath. She ran her thumb over his full lips, tightened with emotion, by fear for her. His hair was a bit shorter, but still with one recalcitrant lock that fell onto his forehead. She remembered running her hands through that hair on the night of their senior prom. A normal teenage night when they had snuck off to a beach in Biscayne and made love for the first time.

"Alex?" She gave in to those memories and raked her hand through his hair.

Her action released his restraint. He dragged her close and kissed her. A kiss that held nothing back.

She didn't run from it, didn't back away. She tried to reach for the love she had once had for him. Love reborn from the ashes of what they used to have. A love for the future filled with security and possibility.

She urged herself into the kiss, exploring the contours of his lips, opening her mouth and inviting him in. She wanted the heat they had once shared. But as hard as she tried, it didn't happen. The fire just wasn't there. No matter how much familiarity called to her heart, a bigger piece of it belonged to Ryder. Perhaps it always would.

It wasn't right to mislead Alex. He deserved a woman who could give him all of herself. She wasn't that woman.

Alex must have sensed her reticence, for he tempered his kisses and loosened his hold. "There's someone else, isn't there?"

She couldn't deny it. Ryder was between them in spite of her desire to try to forge a life without him.

"There was someone else. Someone who may not be right for me."

"You must still care for him a lot if, being Mr. Wrong and all, you can't forget him." Alex withdrew and tucked his hands into the pockets of his jeans.

"I…" She stopped, struggling with the feelings she couldn't deny. "He is definitely Mr. Wrong, but yes, I care for him. A lot. Maybe more than I should."

Strange, but saying it seemed to lift a great weight off her shoulders. And the relief only confirmed that she couldn't be with Alex. "I'm sorry. I never meant to hurt you."

He shook his head. "As hard as it is to know it can never be, you didn't hurt me."

She laughed harshly and cupped his cheek, her touch that of a friend and not a lover. "Yes, I did. Years ago, when I pushed you away. I'm sorry because…"

He knew without her finishing. "Can you see yourself growing old beside him?"

She imagined herself growing old, but unfortunately, Ryder wouldn't. Ever. He would be forever young, while she would be old and crinkly. Dead.

"Diana?"

"I don't see myself growing old with *you*. You deserve more than me."

"Actually, you deserved more from me. When you needed me the most, I ran." A slump entered his strong shoulders.

"No, Alex. It wasn't like that at all." She slipped her thumb over his lips when he would have continued his protest. "You tried, harder than I did. But I kept pushing you away. You did all you could."

A sad smile came to his face, as if he recognized the truth in her words. "I wish I'd tried harder."

A small part of her wished he had, as well. If

he had, her life might be different today. But then she never would have met Ryder.

Ryder. Thoughts of him echoed through her skull, unwilling to be pushed away this time. He was a part of her life. Forever, no matter how many times she tried to deny it. She realized then, that unlike Alex, Ryder loved her enough to keep on trying. But then again, Ryder had a luxury Alex didn't possess—time eternal.

"He's a lucky guy," Alex said.

"We need to discuss the case," she said, anxious to finish what had to be done.

"Something's really wrong if Martinez and Moreno are dead." Alex motioned her in the direction of the food.

Haltingly, between forkfuls of lukewarm *tamales,* she filled him in on what had happened. In turn, Alex provided her with details of the information passed down by the unit leaders and the general impressions he had gotten from the few lower level CDA soldiers he'd come into contact with during the course of the day.

"We're going to have to release Lopez."

"He might lead us to the weapon. If someone doesn't clue him in to our next move."

"If it isn't you or me, and I don't think my partner or the ADIC are responsible—"

"What about the N.Y.P.D.?"

"Never. I trust Daly without question."

Alex considered her for a moment. "Is he the one?"

The one? It took a moment for the question to register. "No, he's not. We've worked together before and he's a friend. A trusted friend."

"Which leaves us with who? Rupert?"

She wrinkled her nose and her disgust must have been obvious.

"Okay, so he doesn't play well with others. I know that, but does that make him a mole?"

Alex had a valid point. A good part of her unease around Rupert revolved around personal dislike. Nothing so far pointed to his being anything other than a trusted member of the team. "If it isn't him—"

"I didn't say that, did I? He rubs me wrong, as well. I just thought it was because of his abrasive manner."

"So what do we do? Investigate him?"

"We need to get the information somehow."

To get Rupert's file through official channels

would be difficult and would likely alert Rupert to their concerns. Unofficial channels meant adding people to the loop. Those people would need to be people who could be trusted. David had some connections he had used in the past, and he suspected Rupert, as well. "My partner can help."

Alex nodded around a mouthful of rice and beans. "I might be able to call in some favors."

Which covered the Rupert possibility, but not the others. "From now on, only the top level gets information in advance. The rest of the agents will be on a need-to-know basis. Agreed?"

"Agreed. Lopez has to have moved the weapon. When we know where, we don't tell anyone else until we're at the location."

Diana rose. "Now that that's settled, if you don't mind, there's something else I have to do tonight."

"If you need me—"

"I know you're here and I truly appreciate your friendship." She hoped her words would make it clear to him where their relationship stood.

Just as she had to decide where her relationship with Ryder was headed.

She exited the safe house and slipped into her car. Pulling her cell phone off her belt, she dialed Ryder's home number. When there was no answer, she knew she had no choice but to search the night for him.

Chapter 19

Nearly midnight and the Lair was hopping. Diana threaded her way through the crowd and opened her senses to try to connect with Ryder, but failed to establish any kind of bond. Eventually she worked her way past the gyrating throng to the bar.

Meghan, the young vamp Blake had turned last year, was there. "You filling in?"

Meghan smiled and, without Diana even asking, poured a shot of Cuervo.

Diana picked up the glass and socked back the shot. The tequila burned its way down her throat and immediately warmed the nearly empty bowl of her belly. "Whew. That has a kick."

"Boss man's not here," Meghan said as she picked up the bottle of Cuervo.

Diana covered the mouth of her glass with her hand. "Thanks, but no. I need my wits tonight."

"Especially if you're headed to the Blood Bank." She whisked away the empty shot glass and replaced it with a diet Coke.

Diana took a sip of the soda. "And I would be on my way to the Blood Bank because Ryder's there?"

With a shrug of her fine-boned shoulders, Meghan tilted her head to one side. "You didn't hear it from me, but Ryder goes there way too much lately."

"Since…me?"

"Since he became our friend, but more now. Yes, maybe since the thing with you."

It didn't take a rocket scientist to see thoughts of the Blood Bank bothered Meghan. "Is that where Blake—"

"Sired me? Yes. In one of the back rooms." She looked at the slick steel counter, where she trailed her finger through the condensation from Diana's glass.

Diana remembered the back room well, having shared some time there with Ryder during their last crime-solving endeavor. With a last sip of her soda, she reached into her pocket and withdrew a twenty. "Thanks for the information."

"I can't take money from—"

"A friend? Thanks, but I'm sure you could use the tip."

A broad smile replaced Meghan's earlier mopiness. "Watch your neck tonight."

With a wave, Diana walked back to her car. If she was headed to the Blood Bank, she wanted to be prepared this time, unlike the last. She opened her glove compartment and removed a spare clip—a special one loaded with silver bullets.

Easing the Glock from her holster, she replaced her regulation clip and tucked her pistol back into the comforting spot beneath her arm. The weight and bulk of the Glock provided a reassuring presence.

She drove the two dozen or so blocks to the Blood Bank and parked the car at the mouth of a small alley. There was a line waiting to enter, but the bouncer smiled, nodded and let her in.

Diego sat next to Blake, watching as Stacia played with a foolish Goth man on the dance floor. She moved her leather-clad body close to his, teasing, making him follow her before retreating. Each step in the dance took them closer and closer to one of the back rooms.

"Five gets you ten she has him there in less than a minute," Blake said, and slapped a bill on the tabletop.

Diego wasn't inclined to take the bet, seeing as how he expected Stacia to accomplish the task in less time than that. She seemed edgy tonight. Determined to make up for the fact that Ryder had vacated the premises the moment she'd walked through the door. If the wannabe with her had any sense, he'd leave before he became Stacia's midnight snack.

"Whoa, mate. Trouble at two o'clock."

Diego whipped his head in that direction. *Dios,* but there would certainly be trouble if Diana and Stacia ran into each other. He rose from his seat, but Blake grabbed hold of his arm.

"No way, mate. This has to play itself out."

Blake was right. It was too late.

Stacia had seen Diana and had stopped her dalliance with the Goth. Diana, likewise, paused and turned in the direction of the dance floor, as if sensing Stacia.

So Ryder had bitten her? That was the only explanation for why Diana could detect the other vampire. Interesting and very surprising, Diego thought.

The two women stood there, eyeballed each other across the distance. Barely the click of a second hand passed before they hesitantly approached one another.

"Five gets you ten that Diana—"

"Shut up, Blake." Diego found nothing amusing about a confrontation between these two women. If anything happened to Diana…

If anything was going to happen to anyone, it might be to Stacia. "No interest, Blake," he said, but from behind them, another voice intruded.

"Yum. A cat fight. I'll take that bet." Foley dropped a five on the tabletop with a lascivious look as the two women finally stood face-to-face.

"A fool and his money are soon parted," Diego warned, and settled back in his chair to watch the show.

Diana examined the woman—no, make that vampire—standing in front of her. The energy pushed off the vamp's body, surging toward Diana. They were of a like height and coloring, but the vampire was dressed in black leather that fit like a second skin and allowed toned muscles to ripple as she moved. Her exotic eyes—as black as midnight—flitted over Diana with a mix of amusement and puzzlement.

"So you're her," the vamp said, her tones cultured and with an accent Diana couldn't place.

"And you would be?"

"Stacia." The vampire took a step closer, as if in a dare.

Diana didn't budge even though the vamp's nearness brought the scent of orange blossoms and provoked unwelcome emotions. A mix of fear—her own—and desire—the vamp's. The power she had sensed earlier brought her body to a painful arousal as Stacia closed the distance between them and wrapped an arm around Diana's waist. Her nipples tightened and her body throbbed and clenched, on the edge of a climax.

As their gazes connected, Stacia said, "Ryder is afraid that when death calls for you, he won't be able to let you go."

Diana slipped one hand up to Stacia's shoulder, needing something to hold on to as desire grew within her, making her dizzy and weak. "How do you know?"

The image conquered her mind. Stacia riding him. Her hips shifting. Between Diana's own legs, the familiar feel of Ryder filled her and her breath exploded from her chest. "Bitch," she said roughly, even as her knees trembled from the climax threatening to overwhelm her.

"Naughty, naughty, love. I only did it because he was so intrigued." Stacia laid her cheek against Diana's. "You were all he thought of, love. All he wanted while I fucked him."

Control, Diana thought. She couldn't let this vamp toy with her any longer.

Diana filled her mind with images of Ryder.

"Yes, that's it. Think about him with all his delicious honor, beloved. Think about taking him. About the two of us sharing him," Stacia urged.

In Diana's mind, visions exploded again, only this time it was of her and Ryder making love. Ryder kissing her, touching her. It was almost as if she was there, with him. Only suddenly, Stacia was there, as well. Sliding into bed with them. Naked.

Diana moaned as Stacia's fangs grazed her

neck. She tried to fight her way out of the illusion Stacia had created, out of the web of power imprisoning her. Vaguely she recalled the other night, when she had failed to connect with Ryder, remembered the sadness and pain that had closed her mind off to his; Sylvia and her baby, her father's blood staining her hands and his last whisper of breath, Alex's retreating back as he'd walked away a decade earlier.

Now, with each bitter memory, the desire fled until she was able to rip away from Stacia's mind games to reality, to the feel of cold lips against her neck as Stacia licked the invisible scar of Ryder's bite.

"You need our emotion, don't you, Stacia?" Diana eased one hand between their bodies.

Stacia, still caught in the throes of the passion she had been broadcasting, mistook the action. "Touch me, beloved. Touch me like he touched me." Her words were part order, but greater part plea. For a moment Diana pitied the vamp.

The vamp's twisted need made it possible for Diana to hastily shift her hand, slip out her Glock and place it directly above Stacia's heart.

Stacia stiffened and inched back enough to

take note of the threat. She smiled, seemingly amused. "Do you think that will stop me?"

Diana laughed harshly. "Silver, Stacia. It will slow you down. And stop you if you can't get someone to dig it out in time."

The vamp's smile faded. "That might be a big ouch."

"Glad you understand that. Not to mention that Foley would get upset if we made a mess on his dance floor."

Stacia glanced to the side of the room and Diana followed her gaze to where Diego, Blake and Foley sat at a table. Foley was handing Blake some money.

"Boys will be boys," Stacia said.

As Diana looked at the vamp once more, a sense of connection arose, different from the one before. "You can say that again."

Stacia narrowed her eyes. "United we stand, is that it, *amiga?*"

Diana's gun was still trained on Stacia's heart, but she knew that wouldn't protect her forever. Taking a gamble that the other woman wanted her alive more than dead, she eased the gun back into her holster and held out her hand for a truce.

Shock flashed across Stacia's features before

she gave Diana a sexy knowing smile that promised much much more than friendship. "You're not my type."

In her head, Diana heard, *But you and Ryder are definitely mine. In time,* amiga. *In time.*

Stacia whirled away, but then quickly turned back. "Neat little trick, breaking free like that. Just a word of warning—it doesn't work the same with every vamp." Stacia inclined her head in the direction of the male vampires nestled together, still watching them intently. "Foley, for instance. He just loves feeding on all that turmoil."

"Thanks for the warning."

Stacia nodded and walked away, her swaying hips drawing the attention of nearly every male in the place, both alive and undead.

Diana chuckled and shook her head, finding Stacia disturbingly interesting. Like Ryder had, it suddenly occurred to her, bringing anger and pain that the two had shared—

He didn't know. Stacia met Diana's gaze across the width of the room. Diana inclined her head in acknowledgment and again went in search of Ryder.

Chapter 20

The doorman at Ryder's apartment, familiar with her, allowed her entry into the building. She hurried upstairs, wondering whether her night would be a total bust, but as she neared the duplex penthouse, she sensed Ryder's loneliness and confusion.

She paused at the door, cautious, thinking about how she could tell him all that she had to say.

"Why don't you start with 'Hello'?" he said as he threw open the door.

It had only been weeks since she'd seen him and yet it seemed like forever. Emotion nearly overwhelmed her. He was standing there, within easy reach if she could muster the courage.

"Hello." The hesitant catch in her voice brought a crooked grin to his lips.

"Hello to you, too. Care to come in? Have some wine?" He raised the glass he held.

"That would be nice." Although "nice" could in no way describe anything about them or their relationship.

Ryder stepped aside and motioned her to the balcony. On a table next to an oversize chaise lounge sat a bottle of wine and an empty glass.

"Waiting for someone?" she asked, surprisingly annoyed by the prospect that he might have been expecting Stacia.

"Jealous?" One dark brow arched upward, a prominent slash against his pale face as he poured a glass of wine for her.

She could have kept playing games, but it wasn't her style. So she pulled up the memory Stacia had left with her, let it fill her mind and reach out to his.

"Shit." Ryder crashed down onto the chaise, causing it to grate against the stone floor of the terrace.

She allowed the vision to clear and met Ryder's disgusted gaze. "She messed with your mind." Her hands trembled as she held the glass up to her lips.

"I'll kill the bitch."

She knew he meant it. Knew that in the world he was melding into, such violence was routine unless...

"Don't go there, please. Don't become like the rest of them."

"Why not?" He spread his hands out and motioned to the night around them. "This is where I belong, darlin'. Creature of the night and all."

His face, silvered by the moonlight, was harshly defined, the lines of his features sharp. His fangs were even sharper and his eyes glowed with the unnatural phosphorescent light of the demon.

"This is what I am. What I will be forever," he reminded her, but she couldn't fail to hear the self-loathing behind his words.

She took another sip of her wine and reached across him to place the glass on the table. She wanted to show him she wasn't afraid. The demon might have driven her away, but she was back. Her time in the human world, with its own darkness, had taught her that she could deal with that part of him.

Really, love? He brushed those lethal fangs along the fragile skin of her neck, which brought a shiver of fear and need.

"It won't work, Ryder. You can't scare me away."

"I thought I had. I thought that was why you needed the space."

Uncertainty almost replaced her earlier resolve, until she ran her thumb along the edges of his mouth and the dangerous fangs, then locked her gaze with his. "I *was* afraid. *Of me.* The world you showed me… So cruel at times. So black-and-white and yet… It called to me. To the way I was or maybe still am."

"It isn't a nice world."

"No, it isn't, but neither is my human one. The path I've chosen is hard and filled with violence. But if I didn't follow that path, I'd be denying a part of what I am."

"Are you sure—"

"I'm sure of how much being with you balances me. How it drives the worst of the darkness away."

The demon fled with her words. When Ryder spoke again, he was human, his dark eyes filled with emotion, his full lips soft beneath her thumb. "And so now you want—"

"To talk. To let you know what I feel because—"

"Dealing with this whole undead thing beats a normal life?" He leaned forward and sniffed. "I can smell him, you know. He's all over you."

She thought of Stacia. "Can we not do this?"

"I'm sorry. And I'm sorry about what happened with Stacia. I didn't—"

She raised her hand to silence him. "I'd like to kick her ass, but I'm smart enough to know I can't. Yet."

"I'm sorry about what happened with her."

"It hurts. A lot. It hurts only a little less since you didn't know, only… Why did you go to her? Why the fascination?"

He laughed harshly. Shifting away from her, he pillowed his head in his hands and looked up at the night sky. "She's been alive for nearly two thousand years. I thought that in all that time, she might have learned how to deal with it."

"With what, Ryder?" Uninvited, she joined him on the chaise, lying on her side next to him.

"With death. With the thought of one day losing you. With the power to take or give life."

Ryder fixed his gaze on the moon and held his

breath, not sure how she would react. She closed the last distance between them, laid her head on his shoulder and placed her hand on his chest. It was more than he had hoped for, and, in truth, more than he deserved.

You deserve more, amor. "You deserve someone who can love you forever. And I'm not that person. In the past few weeks, I've had to face death more than I might have liked and yet…" She took a breath and closed her eyes, clearly struggling. "I don't think I'm strong enough to live with everyone leaving me, even if you're by my side."

Pain gripped his gut, twisting it into a painful knot. "I'm not sure I can let you go."

Diana raised up on one elbow. "Stacia said that's why you went to her. Did it help?"

He laughed harshly. "Actually, it only made me realize how long eternity can be without someone to share it with."

"Ryder—"

He laid a finger on her lips to silence her. "When the time comes…I may not be able to let you die."

"You will, Ryder. You're an honorable man and if you promise me—"

"I don't know if I can. And I can't ever give you—"

"When Sylvia told me she was pregnant, I imagined how my life might be different. Then Alex came back. I thought that if it could be the way it was, before my dad died, I could have that different life. A nice house somewhere, filled with a kid or two. Time for a husband and job, as well. Women do it every day, right?"

"Right," he said, as if he hated agreeing with her.

"Only I'm not the girl I was before my dad died. I guess I knew that all along, but having Alex here…"

"Brought it home?" he asked.

She nodded and lay back down, her head on his shoulder, hand over his heart. "Sylvia. My dad. Thinking about their deaths made me realize that what counts is not how long a life you live, but how full of life you are while you're alive."

Ryder thought of his own lives, both human and vampire. Thought of how he hadn't truly lived until Diana had come into his existence. How being with her made him feel complete.

"That's how you make me feel, Ryder. Complete. I could have a mortal life with Alex or with someone else, but a part of me—a big part of me—would be empty without you."

Was she thinking of what his life would be like after her death? Whether his life would have an empty place without her?

"Diana, look at me." He gently urged her to meet his gaze. Her eyes glistened with tears and one slowly trailed down her face. "Being without you—"

"I don't know if I can stay without a promise that you won't turn me."

He closed his eyes and took a deep breath, imagined never holding her again, never kissing her. He thought about what she had said about living as full a life as one could. As long as his life had been, emptiness had ruled for far too long.

Cradled in his hands was the face of the one person who could change that, if only for a short moment in his existence. How could he lose the prospect of even that short span of happiness? "I promise." He brushed her lips with his as he repeated it. "I promise, Diana."

A sigh escaped her lips, bathed him with her

relief. "Thank God, 'cause I wasn't sure I could leave."

Her honesty dragged a laugh from him and he kissed her once again. "So what do we do now?"

Diana shifted her body over his. "It hasn't been that long that you've forgotten, has it?" She moved her body, wanting to drive away thoughts of anything else. Anyone else.

He clearly read her mind. As he wrapped his arms around her waist, he whispered, "There's only one person in my heart. Only one person I ever thought of, no matter what Stacia made me do."

She eased away from him. "I know that. I want you to know that I didn't—"

"It wouldn't matter to me if you did, darlin'," he said.

"Liar. But I didn't."

A smile erupted on his face a second before he reclaimed her lips. But when he made a motion as if to rise from the chaise, she muttered, "No. Right here."

"Here?" His hands sneaked beneath the hem of her suit jacket, eased her shirt out of her pants and slipped beneath to feel skin, alive with mortal warmth.

She shot a look at the full moon, which bathed them with the kiss of her light. "You are a creature of the night, aren't you? Besides, it's been too long. I don't want to wait."

He groaned at her words and at the way she straddled his hips, shifted herself along the length of him. The very erect length of him.

"Ryder?"

He placed his hands at her waist to still her movements. "I don't want to wait, either."

Smiling, she yanked at her suit jacket, but winced as the movement brought pain to her injured shoulder.

"Diana?"

"There was a shootout today—" Immediately he undid the buttons on her shirt to reveal the fist-size bruise a few inches beneath her left collarbone.

"Christ, Diana. You could have been…" He laid his hand over the wound and dragged the pads of his fingers over the highly sensitive area.

The action yanked a gasp from her.

"Did I hurt you?"

"Never." As her gaze locked with his, he realized the sound had been one of desire. Gently he shifted to ease her holster and shirt from her body. Then he undid the clasp on her bra. Her nipples hardened immediately.

"Can I touch you?" He waited for her nod before finally cradling her breasts in his hands. He passed his thumbs over the peaks of her nipples. She wanted nothing more than for him to touch her harder.

"Do you want me to bite?" He moved his mouth to the tip of one breast.

She slipped her hand to the nape of his neck and urged him close. "A love bite, not—"

"*The* bite. To be turned, you have to put the bite on me, after…"

His pause made her pull away from him. "After what?"

"After I drain you or…"

Despite his hesitation she knew. "I'm dying. You promised not to turn me and I trust that promise because—"

"If we don't have trust between us, what do we have?"

She nodded and laid her head against his. "Love me, Ryder. Bite me. A human bite."

He eased his hand to the middle of her back

and held her to him as he licked the tip. Her breath grew more uneven with each pull until he finally bit down, creating a clenching need between her legs. She rubbed that need against his erection, but she didn't want to rush. Didn't want all the feelings to evaporate with a sexual climax.

Wrapping her arms around him, she held him close, accepting the way he loved her with his mouth until she was trembling, hot, wanting to kiss and suck and bite him, as well.

She eased her hands between them and took off his shirt. When his skin came into contact with hers, it was cold.

Rubbing the hard little buttons of his nipples, she smiled at his surprised sigh of pleasure. "Do you like?"

Ryder leaned back so she would have greater access to his body. "Will you bite?" he asked, a wry smile on his face.

"Only if you ask me to."

"Bite me."

Laughing, she bent her head and tongued one dark copper nipple before closing her teeth around the tip and gently giving him the kind of bite she had known he wanted.

Ryder groaned and cupped her head, loving the feel of her perfect white teeth, which she moved to the side of his neck.

He held her head to him and urged his hips against her as she gave him the mother of all hickies, her sweet mouth pulling and sucking on his skin, making his erection swell almost painfully in the confines of his jeans. Making the demon wake as it imagined sucking and biting at her.

He battled to keep the demon away and Diana raised her head.

"You're getting warmer."

"It's…hard," he said, struggling, especially when she ground her hips against him and teased, "Yes, it is."

"Darlin', stop." He grasped her hips to still the motion.

"Stacia said you were afraid of your demon. Of what it could do," she said, and sank down onto him, the tight tips of her breasts rubbing his chest.

"I am afraid, Diana. I don't know if—"

"I trust you."

A shudder ripped through his body at her faith in him and for the longest time, they lay there together, caught in the midst of passion unfulfilled.

Then she inched up his body to kiss him. The kiss one of tenderness, of apology. It tempered that earlier, almost uncontrollable desire. The passion the kiss created grew slowly, carefully, as they both realized the fine edge they walked whenever they were together.

When they finally broke apart, Diana fingered his nipple again and he did the same in a sexy game of follow the leader. She smiled at that thought, and lowered her hand to trace the defined edges of his abdomen; he ran the pad of his finger along her midsection.

Sensation skittered along her nerves and she flattened her palm on the paleness of his abdomen, made even milkier white by the revealing moonlight.

A breeze brought with it the sounds of the city below. Sounds that failed to mask the groan she drew from him as she unzipped his jeans, slipped her hands beneath his briefs and covered him with her hand. Nor did the city's clamor obscure her own gasp as he copied her actions and found the center of her.

As she stroked, he stroked, her gaze locked on his as his was on hers. The pupils of his eyes dilated with desire and his breath grew as rough as hers until she bent her head and kissed him again.

"Ryder!" He knew, for he helped her completely undress, until all that remained was a lacy scrap of panties around the fullness of her hips.

Ryder slowly inched the panties down her legs, pausing as he did so to drop kiss after kiss. First on her knee, then on an ankle and, finally, on his way back up, on the tender inside of her thigh.

He smiled as his body lay cradled between her legs. Ryder exerted the barest hint of pressure to part her thighs and brushed his nose against the soft patch of dark curls at the center of her. She raised her hips and tangled her hand in his hair in invitation.

He darted his tongue out to taste the muskiness of her desire. She murmured her pleasure and he sucked at the hard nub, licking downward until he could slip his tongue within her to savor her need for him.

She called out his name and he knew she didn't want to wait anymore. Nor did he.

He surged upward, drawing his pants down enough to free himself and then he was in her, in that wet he had just tasted. She was tight around him as he drew out of her. The friction of their bodies made him increase the tempo of his loving. She responded, lifting her thighs to hold his hips, grasping his shoulders as he escalated the force of his thrusts, driving her upward on the chaise, drawing a shocked breath from her.

"Are you okay?"

Her breath was ragged, her hands on his shoulders tight as she said, "I'm okay and you're…human still."

He was. In all that time, the demon had barely registered. He didn't really understand why. Maybe he didn't want the beast there. He wanted to stay human and feel her response, feel her love as she held him.

"I want to be normal for you. I want to give you what you deserve."

Diana wrapped her arms around his shoulders. As he drove into her, she moaned with the pleasure he created, and told him what was in her heart. "You are what I deserve, Ryder. You are all that I could ever need, *querido*."

At her words, he came, spilling himself inside of her, his big body shuddering with his release.

She cradled him as he wrapped his arms around her and shifted so that she was lying on top of him, still joined.

"I'm sorry, darlin'. I—"

"Shh, *amor.* Just kiss me." He did, his mouth tender on hers, conveying all that he was feeling: his need for her, his satisfaction in her arms.

She answered each kiss, experiencing in his arms what she hadn't with Alex. Peace. Conflict. Need. Solace. The yin and yang that she so desperately needed. Dark and light. Diana and Ryder.

He grew hard again within her and she moved on him. He caressed her breasts, then replaced his hands with his mouth until the joy he brought her overwhelmed her and she cried out his name as she came.

Chapter 21

There were long hours to fill before her team assembled for the raid, hours that Diana didn't want to spend in her office worrying. Tonight wasn't going to be easy with no one to trust. David would be in a command post and Alex would be within the apartment. ADIC Hernandez wouldn't be there and they had opted to keep the N.Y.P.D. out of this operation.

The men who would be beside her were unknowns, and Rupert seemed too keen to see her fail.

She wanted to see Ryder before tonight's raid. Just for a few hours…

Okay, so she was spooked about tonight. Sick with worry that things might go horribly wrong. She forced herself not to think about it as if by doing so it wouldn't come to pass. But if it did…

She had told Ryder that what mattered in life was not the quantity, but the quality of it. How well life had been lived.

She intended to live it to the fullest before tonight.

In less than an hour, she was at Ryder's apartment. The door opened and he stood there, looking sexy with his sleep-rumpled hair and bare chest. Silk pajama bottoms rode low on his lean hips. "Thought I felt you." He opened the door wide in welcome.

"Keeping vamp hours now?"

"Actually, trying to catch up on some sleep. Didn't get much last night," he replied with a cocky grin.

Heat flared to her face. She was the reason for his lack of sleep. After they'd moved indoors, dawn had crept into the sky before she'd finally closed her eyes for some rest.

"I'm kinda tired myself," she admitted, unable to voice her real reasons for coming here.

Ryder appraised her carefully, but didn't challenge her. Instead he slipped his hand around her nape and drew her close. "Well, if you have some time, why not take a nap with me?"

A nap, she thought, had been the furthest thing from her mind. But lying beside him, snuggled in his arms for a few hours might bring peace to her troubled mind. "I'd like that."

"Good." With his arm wrapped around her shoulders, he walked her to his bedroom. He immediately slipped into bed, but propped his head on one arm to watch her as she undressed.

It was unnerving to be the sole focus of his attention.

"Can you not watch?"

"I like to watch. See the shields come down."

"Shields, huh?" She babied her shoulder by removing one side of her holster first and then easing off the other. The Glock didn't make a sound as she carefully placed it on the carpet.

"You change when the suit and weapons come off."

His words stopped her in the midst of unbuttoning her blouse. "What?"

He snared her waist and pulled her into the vee of his legs. As he removed her blouse, he explained, "You're always a warrior, darlin'. But without the de rigueur suit and those deadly little toys of yours…" His breath spilled against the skin just above her breasts a second before he undid the clasp of her bra.

"Ryder?"

Her answer, in part, was the way he swept beneath the parted fabric and cupped her breasts, dragging a shaky breath from her. They were still sensitive, so tender that just the touch of his hands drew her nipples into stiff nubs.

"Ryder," she repeated, only this time she wanted something else.

"You're more human with the defenses down, darlin'." He rubbed his goatee across the tip of one breast and then across the other.

She grasped the back of his head and kissed his forehead. "I thought you said you wanted to take a nap."

Not that she was going to stop him as he dropped a kiss on the spot right above her heart.

"You need to finish undressing." He kept his hands at her waist as she toed off her shoes and tossed aside her ankle holster to rest against its big brother.

It was then he moved to the center of the bed where he pillowed his head on his hands. "Ready for that nap?"

His position displayed the lean muscles of his chest and abdomen to perfection. No centerfold could come close to the sexiness he exuded, especially when he smiled, displaying perfectly white and totally human teeth. And of course, there was his erection, admirably tenting the silk of his pajama bottoms and bringing a rush of damp to private parts still tender from last night. But not so tender that she couldn't imagine…

Nap time, he reminded her. In his eyes was the promise of so much more.

She eased into the bed and slipped her thigh over his hard length, dragging a moan from him.

"Nap time," she teased.

"Payback's a bitch, isn't it?"

He wanted her. Badly. Wanted to keep her there until morning when she would be safe. Not that she would stay. She was his warrior and she was needed in the mortal world. She was one of the good guys and she wouldn't run from her obligations, even when she worried they might kill her. He could sense the fear emanating from her, perceive the distress clouding her mind.

Solace was the reason she had come to him, he suspected. It made him tighten his hold on her.

"You okay?" he asked, not that he expected truth-fulness. She'd always kept her feelings from him.

Her long hesitation was followed by the tenta-tive caress of her hand over his heart. Then she surprised him. "I'm worried about tonight. About a raid I need to go on."

He placed one hand on her determined little chin and applied delicate pressure to raise her face. "I can be there. Watch out for you."

She shook her head. "It's okay. I think I'm just being paranoid."

Ryder was sure that her concerns were anything but paranoia. Her self-control wouldn't let an emotion like that fester. "Trust your gut, darlin'. Trust me to be there and make sure that—"

She covered his lips with her hand. "I don't want to talk about this anymore. *Por favor.*"

As he'd thought, she'd come to him for refuge from her everyday world. He intended to give it to her. "Then let's talk about…us."

"Us? As in—"

"You and me. Together. Here."

Diana shook her head, confused until he clari-fied his statement. "As in, together more often. As in you staying here with me, sharing a bed and the closet and the dresser." Tension crept into his body as he waited for her to answer.

"As in me living here? With you?"

"Look, I know it's not really living with me 'cause I'm not living, but…I want to be with you. All the time. I want to go to sleep beside you. Wake up beside you."

Diana knew there were still many unresolved issues between them. In time, they would have to deal with their fears about her mortality and the brutality of the vampire world that surrounded them. But his attempt to provide a small sliver of normalcy in the midst of that was something she couldn't refuse.

She smiled. "I'd like the same thing."

He grinned then, his smile bright against the dark hair of his goatee. "So where do we start?"

"Start?"

"Hmm." He cupped her breasts and her nipple peaked against the palm of his hand.

The desire that had already been simmering between them flared to life. "That's a good start."

He kissed the tip of her other breast, rubbed his beard against it. "And this? Is this good, also?"

She raked her fingers into the long strands of his hair and held him to her breasts. "That's an even better start."

"Good." He finally took her into his mouth and suckled her. His actions were gentle, slow, building passion bit by bit as if to reinforce that they had all the time in the world.

Only they didn't, she thought as she kissed him back, thinking of tonight. If this was going to be the last thing she ever did with him, she wanted it to be perfect. She wanted to give him all of herself, without restraint, without any doubts.

She tempered her own response, banking her need so that there wasn't a spot on him she didn't caress. She told him with her hands and her mouth what she still couldn't with words—that he was the only man in her world who could fill the empty spots in her heart and make her happy.

They were both trembling, breaths rasping unevenly when he sat up and grasped her waist, slipped inside her. She held him to her as if he was the only stable thing in her world. Which he was. Always.

Ryder buried his head between her breasts, his

ear pressed in the gap above her heartbeat, erratic with their passion, madly beating with life. "I love you, Diana. Forever."

She smiled. "I love you, too. I can't imagine my life without you."

Which unfortunately brought him a vision of life without her, of losing her. *Possibly tonight,* came the thought broadcast by the fear within her.

Not tonight, darlin'. Not tonight.

No, not tonight. She gripped him more tightly.

He opened himself to her so that their thoughts merged and became one in much the same way their bodies were already one.

"Not even death will keep me from loving you."

As the words echoed in his skull, he didn't know which of them had said the words. It didn't matter. He was a part of her soul as she was his. Her love was the only thing that had sustained him in more than a century of existence.

He wouldn't allow anything to take that away from him.

Chapter 22

The teams loaded on the bus had no idea of where they were going. Only she, her ADIC, David and Rupert knew.

And Alex. After their last talk, she had no doubts he would guard her back.

At the lower West Side location—a condemned apartment building slated for demolition—she instructed the team on their positions.

Rupert and one other agent had taken the roof of the building across from the apartment. David and two others manned a command center in a lower floor of that building while a half-dozen other agents surrounded the location to safeguard anyone escaping the raid. Which left her and two other agents to break through the door of the apartment where Alex and two other CDA members were supposed to be guarding the weapon.

After the team dispersed, Diana slipped her wire into her ear. "David."

"Clear as a bell. We've got an unobstructed view. All other units check in." One by one, each unit confirmed that they were in place.

Unlike the two agents with her, she wasn't wearing full body armor, only her vest and an FBI windbreaker. The armored agents would break through the door before she entered, just as they now took the point, sweeping ahead of her through the deserted building.

They moved swiftly to a dark stairwell that smelled of urine and the refuse left by assorted squatters. By the fifth floor, she was sweating, but it wasn't from the climb. She was too physically fit for that. The cold sweat of fear made her palms damp and twisted her insides as they slowly approached the apartment.

She raised her fisted hand to signal the other two agents to stop. Across the way, she noted a dim light. David and the two other agents were there.

Her partner confirmed his presence by saying, "We've got you in sight."

She glanced toward the roof. A fleeting burst

of light, like that from a muzzle, caught her attention for a moment, but then Rupert's voice came across the line. "All ready, Reyes."

Turning to the two men with her, she could see nothing in the face masks they wore aside from her own pale reflection. A line of sweat dripped down the middle of her back. Her heartbeat skipped in an awkward rhythm as she motioned for them to assume their positions.

Taking a place beside one of the men, she called out, "FBI. Open the door."

Silence greeted her.

She repeated the warning, louder and more forcefully than before. "FBI! Open the door!"

Again there was no hint of activity. With a wave of her hand, the two agents picked up the small battering ram they had dragged up the stairs.

They needed space to swing the heavy compact tool. She stepped back, toward the ledge of the open-air hall to give them room and prepare herself for a running start into the apartment.

What was Alex doing? Why hadn't he answered? But as they began the countdown, she let everything fall from her mind except the job at hand.

"One. Two—"

A blow to her back rocked her as blinding pain ripped through her chest. Her knees buckled, only she didn't fall. Someone grabbed her from behind. She barely had time to register what was happening as she heard a grunt and searing fire erupted in her midsection.

Before her fading vision, explosions of bright red stained the dull gray paint of the building's wall. Her feet tripped over something as she was propelled forward, toward the door.

She managed to get her hands up, protecting herself from the impact. The door burst inward to reveal three men, Alex amongst them, slumped against one wall. His shirtfront was soaked with blood.

Blood, she thought, looking downward and finally noticing something dark and wet coating the front of her vest and flowing over the arm wrapped around her waist.

Ryder's arm, she thought, before blackness claimed her.

Ryder stumbled to the back of the apartment, past the dead and dying men.

His strength failed him. He'd been shot. He vaguely recollected the blow when he'd blocked her body with his. He'd failed to protect her.

He crumpled against the far wall of the apartment, cradling Diana in his arms. She was barely alive.

Taking a deep breath to control the pain from his own wound, he laid her on the ground so that he could get her stabilized until help arrived. As he gently placed her on the floor, he realized there was too much blood. His. Hers. That of the men around them. Sweet, rich and warm on his hands. Heat gathered in his belly and spread outward. He gritted his teeth and closed his eyes, summoning all of his strength to keep the demon away. A difficult battle. Almost as hard as mustering the courage to remove Diana's vest and check the damage.

The blood soaking her shirt was all too obvious. He parted the vest further and muttered a curse.

The demon reawakened, bringing unwanted warmth throughout his body. He battled it back yet again, knowing that if the vampire emerged, he might not be able to control it. He might not be able to keep his promise.

He took a deep breath and looked back at Diana.

She was regaining consciousness, possibly running on pure adrenaline. Her eyelids fluttered open and she grabbed his hand. Sticky blood bound their palms together. She peered at him, confusion clouding the gold-green of her eyes.

"What happened?" Her voice was so low he barely heard her.

"I don't know," he said softly, but she didn't hear his answer as she moaned and closed her eyes, agony evident in every line of her body.

He had planned to get her somewhere safe, but death would find them no matter where they went.

He cradled her in his arms and leaned back against the wall. He murmured soft words of love and reassurance in the hope it would comfort her as she passed. He had no doubt she would not survive the wounds. Already a large wet stain soaked her shirt and the top of her pants. The telltale blackness of the blood confirmed one bullet had hit her liver.

Her eyes opened again, glimmering with tears. She grabbed hold of his shirt, her hands fisted against the fabric. Her perfect white teeth bit her lower lip, drawing yet more blood as she battled the pain. Beneath his hands, her body vibrated with it, shaking as fresh waves of agony buffeted her body.

"Ryder…" she moaned. "S-s-sorry…wasted… time."

"No regrets, darlin'." He stroked her hair.

She surprised him by managing a smile. "No…regrets." The smile faded, replaced by a grimace of pain. "Not…s-s-scared."

He slipped his hand into hers.

"I'm here. I won't leave you alone." He kissed her. A hurried and labored breath came against his lips. Another followed, but not for some time, and even then, it was weaker, shallower. He knew this scenario all too well. He had seen more than one person die over his century of existence. But he had never watched anyone die whom he loved as he did her. Never felt their blood spill onto his hands and against his chest.

Her head tilted back. The hand in his stiffened a second before her body went slack. He pulled her tight against him, wanting her to spend these last moments in his arms, wanting her to not be alone.

Her life's blood spilled out of her body. The heat of it bathed him. Her heartbeat slowed. Softer and less steady until just a slight, hesitant flutter, barely more than the beat of a butterfly's wings, remained.

A sickening wetness bound their bodies from their mutual blood loss, and the smell, that sweet metallic smell, was strong. Too strong.

He didn't have anything left in him to battle the change, nor did he want to. The woman in his arms, her heartbeat nearly gone, could only be saved by one thing and one thing alone.

"Do it, Ryder."

At the words, he ripped his gaze from Diana's pale face to the dark shadow lurking at the door.

"Stacia. What are you—"

"I followed your friends after you called them. You didn't think I'd miss the party, did you?" She sauntered into the room, passing from one body to the next until she stopped by the man he had seen with Diana. "This one's still alive. Unlike your friend will be shortly."

"Leave." Anger surged through his body at Stacia's intrusion. With the anger came the beast, and Stacia laughed.

"Your true face, finally. Suck it up, Ryder. Literally. Turn her or you will never forgive yourself."

"Leave, Stacia," he said, his tone weaker.

"She's almost gone, beloved. Death is calling unless—"

"Stacia, if there ever was a heart in that cold, lifeless body, leave."

A shocked look crept across her features, but she immediately schooled it. "If you love her, you'll keep her with you."

Stacia's parting comment proved hard to ignore. Especially with the demon strong in him, barely leashed. So hard to let her go. *So much easier to turn her,* the demon argued.

But *selfish,* the human countered.

That didn't keep him from burying his head against the barely perceptible pulse point at Diana's neck. Her breath was almost nonexistent, even to his now awakened vamp senses. It wouldn't be much longer, he thought, her pulse lessening while he hesitated, his fangs poised over her artery, over the faint erratic tremble of her blood, sluggishly moving with death so close.

Only a little pressure would be needed to prick

through that delicate skin and taste her. Then she'd feed on him, drawing undead life from the cursed blood flowing through his veins. And yet…

With a loud, hurt-filled moan, he raised his head, nearly howling his frustration. He couldn't do it, even if it meant losing her.

She had asked that he not turn her. Even while knowing she was dying, she had told him she wasn't afraid. Somehow he tapped into that courage. To her strength.

The tears came then, blurring her face, making it easier to imagine life remained. It was the way he wanted to remember her, filled with a vigor and spirit that for a short time had made him happy. Had made him human once again.

Pain colored her world. Each breath required more effort than the one before. Wrong that it should be so draining, that her hands refused to cooperate, losing their tenuous grip on Ryder's shirt, on his hand tucked close to her heart. The edge of her torment was lessened by the strength of him nearby, by the warmth of his body.

Slowly, however, as her breathing became

more and more laborious, a chill set in. She forced herself to draw another breath, but a heavy stone sat on her chest, making even the simple beat of her heart nearly impossible. She struggled for only a little while, and then came a blissful peace that eliminated her agony, ending her useless efforts.

Suddenly she found herself on a beach, the sun glaring brightly. The light called to her, whispering her name until she realized it was no sun. A bright, whirling tunnel of brilliance opened in front of her. From the center a figure emerged, one hand held out in welcome. The light limned the edges of the shape until he left the tunnel and stood before her.

"*Papi?*" Her father came to her, as young as the day he had died.

"*Mi'ja.*" His voice, soft and soothing, dulled the edge of her pain. "I wish it wasn't your time—"

"It can't be, *Papi.*"

"*Hija,*" he began in that voice she recognized from her childhood, the one he had always used with her stubborn side. "I'm here to guide you. We are all waiting for you. Your grandparents and—"

Diana shook her head in denial and took a step back. The pain increased with the movement. Despite that, she retreated from her father's figure. He continued his entreaty, but she balked, turned away and witnessed for the first time the scene below her.

Ryder held her in his arms, his head buried against her neck. The demon. Howling with a pain that sank its teeth deep into her, transferring its anguish. Engulfing her in his loss and yet…

A sense of completeness filled her. She had needed to understand what would make her happy for so long. His love brought the call of her destiny. It wasn't her time. Not yet.

Her father summoned her again. She turned and smiled sadly. "I'm sorry, *Papi,* but I can't go with you now."

She once again looked at Ryder's face, with its elongated fangs and inhuman features. But instead of running from it, she plummeted downward, back into the blinding pool of pain.

Back into his arms.

Chapter 23

Stacia hurried from the room, the tortured energy emanating from Ryder driving her to rage. She had never felt such love, such devotion.

She flew upward onto the roof only to discover she was not alone.

A man stood there, holding some kind of weapon. He whirled, the pleased look on his face vanishing when he noted her vamp features. He was a handsome man, tall, able-bodied. He raised the weapon to his hip and pointed it at her, which only made her laugh.

"Do you think that can hurt me?" She sauntered toward him, moving until the barrel of the weapon nestled against her stomach.

He looked down at the barrel against the bare flesh of her midriff. The heat from the muzzle branded her skin, perfuming the air with the smell of burned flesh.

"It seems to have done fine by me tonight," he said with pride.

Stacia followed his gaze and noted the large fire on one floor, clearly the result of an explosion. Two figures moved along the hallway. Blake and Diego. She had followed them here earlier, but now they were fleeing the flames, dragging someone along with them. She returned her attention to the human.

"Is that your masterpiece?"

A sadistic smile on his face, he replied, "Beautiful, isn't it?"

She thought of Ryder and the woman in his arms, likely dead by now. Another accomplishment of this man.

"You've been a naughty boy." With a quick swipe of her hand, she tore his throat out.

He staggered back, shock on his features as he grabbed at the shredded flesh and cartilage that remained. He tried to speak, but air only whistled through his fingers accompanied by the gurgle of blood. His eyes went sightless while he stood. It took a moment for gravity to drag him to the rooftop.

A human without any humanity. "And they call me a demon." She gave him one final nudge with the point of her black boot to make sure he was truly gone. Satisfied with her handiwork, she leaped to an adjacent rooftop, eager to find a bit of fun to drive away the unpleasantness of the night.

She was sorry that she had ever followed Ryder and his friends.

Ryder rocked back and forth with her in his arms, comforting her as he waited for her to pass, only her heart continued to beat.

Had it stopped? Even for a moment?

He listened. Faint, but still beating. Hanging on.

The delay had given him time to regain some strength, but he wasn't sure he could get Diana somewhere safe, away from whoever was trying to kill her. Somewhere she could receive medical attention.

The sounds of sirens piercing the night told him he didn't have time to linger. Using the wall behind him as a counterbalance, he pushed with his legs and managed to get upright. A wave of weakness swept over him. He'd lost a lot of blood. If he fed from one of the dead men, could he recover the strength he needed?

"You okay, mate?"

At the doorway two figures stood waiting for him. Diego and Blake. He'd called for their help when he'd decided to follow Diana after she'd left his apartment. He'd forgotten about them in all the chaos.

"I can't do this alone."

The two vampires rushed forward, but stopped when they saw his condition and that of the woman in his arms.

"She's in a bad way, *amigo.*" Diego moved to take Diana from him, but Ryder pulled her close, unwilling to give her up for even a second.

"Need to get home." His voice was weak.

Blake laid a hand on his shoulder. "Don't be a stubborn bloke. We can get her to a hospital."

"No hospital. She won't be safe at a hospital." Whoever wanted her dead would search for her and finish the job if they knew she was still alive. He had to leave here. But he couldn't get started, losing his footing from his frailty.

"Bullocks, I knew this was going to be tough,"

Blake said. He looped an arm around Ryder's waist and Diego did the same, giving Ryder the stability he lacked on his own.

Somehow he managed to put one foot in front of the next until they were at the door. Footsteps charging up the stairs urged them to make their escape quickly. His friends used their combined power to get him on the ledge and then up to the roof.

He barely noted the bloody body sprawled on the rooftop. Diego and Blake moved too rapidly, propelling them from one rooftop to the next while he held on to Diana, counting each heartbeat as she clung to life, every second that passed keeping alive his hope that she could somehow survive her injuries.

She was still with him when they reached the balcony and stumbled to the kitchen, where he laid her on the table and dropped into a chair.

"Get Melissa."

Blake left while Diego opened the refrigerator and pulled out a few bags of blood. "Feed," he commanded, and Ryder wasn't about to argue. To keep the demon under control, he needed sustenance.

As he held the bag to his mouth, he grabbed Diana's limp and bloodied hand, breaking contact only when Diego slipped the vest and clothes off her body to expose her wounds.

Maybe it was Ryder's imagination, or possibly his weakness, but it seemed as if the bleeding had slowed. As if the wounds weren't as serious.

Diego balled one towel against her midsection and placed it over the gunshot. "Tight pressure," Ryder instructed. "Tighter." But before Diego could do anything else, Melissa raced into the room, her doctor's bag in hand, Blake and Sebastian behind her. Sebastian cradled something to his chest and Ryder realized it was the baby.

So much for not involving that innocent in his undead life, he thought with disgust. He looked at Diana's still body, wondering why he had ever involved her in his savage world, only…it hadn't been vampire violence that had done this. It had been humans. If not for him and his friends, she'd be dead. Was nearly dead now, he thought as Melissa evaluated Diana's wounds.

"Liver's been compromised. Possibly an artery

in the chest region. I can't deal with this here," Melissa said, shaking her head.

He tossed aside the empty blood bag and said, "You have to. She won't be safe in a hospital."

Sebastian swung around to challenge him. "She's an FBI agent. Of course she'd be safe—"

"Someone on her team did this. They wiped out the two agents with her," Ryder said angrily, the rumble of the animal in his voice.

Sebastian gripped his sister's arm. "Diana," he said softly, but she didn't stir. He looked up at his wife. "Is she going to die?"

"I don't know, but you need to help me." Almost as an afterthought, she said to Ryder, "You need to feed some more. Now."

He was loathe to leave Diana for even a second, but he sensed that his keeper and her husband didn't need his undead demands distracting them. He entered his bedroom and Diego closed the door behind him.

"Feed, and then we must talk, *amigo.*"

Finally releasing the tenuous control he'd been exerting over the demon, Ryder greedily plunged his fangs into another blood bag. As soon as he devoured it, Diego provided yet another. It was only after that last feeding that Ryder finally felt restored.

Falling back against the pillows he had shared just that afternoon with his love, he met Diego's concerned gaze. "I didn't turn her. I promised her I wouldn't."

"Then what happened?"

Ryder searched his memories, trying to piece together what he remembered. "I saw her shot and got behind her to protect her."

There had been pain then. He placed his hand over his injury. "I got shot. The bullet passed through me and into Diana. Through Diana."

"But you didn't bite her?"

Ryder shook his head. "I wanted to. There was so much blood. Her blood. My blood. All over both of us." Could that be what was keeping her alive? he wondered. His blood tainting hers? Seeping into her wounds? "I don't know how she's still alive, but I didn't sire her."

Diego sat on the edge of the bed. "I'm sorry I doubted you, but she's not likely to survive the night. She shouldn't even be alive now."

Ryder battled the pain that came with Diego's words. But the truth couldn't be denied. "I know,

Diego. I want to thank you and Blake for helping me. Without you…"

"Let's not waste any more time here." He offered his hand to help Ryder rise from the bed.

Ryder was steadier than before, with energy singing through his veins from the feeding. When they returned to the kitchen, Melissa had placed pressure bandages on both of Diana's wounds, elevated her legs and covered her with a light blanket.

She was taking Diana's blood pressure, but pulled off her stethoscope when he approached. "She's in a very bad way."

He grasped Diana's hand. Cold to the touch. Damp and with a bluish tinge that spoke of the poor condition of her circulation. Her breathing, although fast, barely moved her chest. Shifting his hand, he took her pulse. Thready and rapid. He had been a doctor once and recognized the symptoms well.

"She's in shock. What can we do?"

"Besides what we're doing? Transfusion. IV drip to replace lost blood volume," Melissa replied, anger in her voice.

"Neither of which we can do here," Sebastian

piped in from where he was sitting at the head of the table, gently brushing his sister's hair with his hand.

"We have to stay here until we know who tried to kill her."

"I'll call my friend Sara. She's working tonight and will be off shortly. She should be able to bring me what we need for the IV drip." Melissa stepped away to phone her friend.

"Maybe Melissa should check you out, as well," Sebastian said.

Ryder glanced down at his shirt, which was soaked with not only Diana's blood but his. He exposed the ragged exit wound, which was already knitting closed. "I'm fine."

Sebastian shot him an accusatory glare.

"I tried to protect her."

"Sucky job," Sebastian said, but quieted as Diana moaned and her eyelids fluttered open.

Ryder leaned close and cradled her cheek. "Diana?"

"Hurts," she murmured, and bit her lower lip. The muscles of her face trembled beneath his hand.

"Rest, darlin'. We're going to make you better."

"Rest." She went slack beneath his hand. When

he grabbed her wrist, her pulse beat a little stronger, slightly steadier.

Melissa returned. "Sara will be here in less than an hour."

"Can she last that long?"

Melissa laid her hand on Diana's neck and took her pulse. "She's here despite all the odds to the contrary. We'll do what we can."

Which was little, Ryder realized as he quickly washed up, changed into clean clothes and returned to Diana's side. They checked the pressure bandages every now and then to stem Diana's blood loss, and though their actions seemed insufficient, her pulse and breathing strengthened. Color tenuously returned to her skin while warmth seeped into her extremities.

Sara arrived as promised, and Melissa rapidly set up the drip to help replace the blood volume Diana had lost. With the IV in place, Diana improved steadily. An hour later, as Melissa checked beneath the pressure bandages, a look of surprise passed over her features.

"What's wrong?" He peered at the most serious of the wounds. The injury appeared smaller. Only a minimal amount of blood leaked from the nearly healed edges, but the blood still bore the telltale black color that spoke of a compromised liver. But the blood loss was nothing compared to what normally occurred with that kind of wound. He pulled away the sheet to examine her abdomen, wondering if she had started to bleed internally. No distension or other bruising appeared. "Help me lift her."

Together, he and Melissa turned Diana on her side so he could examine the corresponding entry wound. Again, it seemed diminished. Here, the blood loss had completely stopped. He shook his head. "I don't get it."

"Don't you?" Sebastian said, accusation thick in his voice.

"Let's get this over with now. I didn't turn her."

"But the way she's healing—"

"Isn't normal," Sebastian finished for his wife.

No, it wasn't. But as Ryder had told Diego earlier, he had no explanation. Didn't really care so long as she was with them. So long as she held on.

The baby started to fuss in Sebastian's arms. The baby he had promised Melissa would have nothing to do with this kind of life. He looked up at the couple and inclined his head in the direction of the door.

"It's time you went home. Got some rest."

Melissa exchanged an uneasy glance with Sebastian. "We're not leaving—"

"Go. I'll call if I need you."

"Ryder."

He silenced her with a wave of his hand. "I was a doctor a long time ago, remember. I think I can handle this."

With a reluctant nod and another glare from Sebastian, he walked them to the door and bid them good-night, confident he could deal with whatever happened. Until midnight, when Diana's temperature spiked and she convulsed on the hard surface of the table.

Ryder covered her body with his, gently restraining her so she wouldn't reopen her wounds. Although she calmed a short time later, the fever remained and climbed higher with each passing hour. She eventually woke, delirious, and rambled about seeing her father.

Unfortunately he vaguely remembered suffering through a similar state—one he had barely survived in the days during which he became a vampire.

Chapter 24

The kitchen table groaned beneath their combined weight. Her body jerked spasmodically beneath his as the fever surged higher and her system reacted violently to the high temperatures.

Ryder held her sweat-drenched head in his hands, trying to keep her from doing too much harm. Long minutes passed before she quieted, her body limp beneath his, her skin slightly cooler thanks to the chill sweat bathing it.

Her eyelids opened a crack, but her eyes were unfocused. Her lips moved as if she was speaking, but only unintelligible murmurs broke the silence of the night.

She was alive.

He told himself that it didn't matter how or why. Only that she was.

Easing off her body now that she was peaceful,

he released the pressure bandage high on her chest—the more manageable of the two wounds, although normally dangerous enough to have been fatal. Beneath the bandage, fresh skin closed the formerly ragged exit wound. No blood escaped. He applied a fresh bandage, making sure it was snug against the healing injury. The damage in the area of her liver had yet to completely heal, but it was on its way. He cleaned it, dressed it and replaced the pressure bandage.

Fearful that another round of spasms would collapse the table, he carried her to his bed, where he left her only long enough to get a basin of ice water and a towel to bathe her heated skin. He had been doing that for a few hours already in the hope of bringing down her temperature.

So far, it hadn't worked. But nothing had helped him after he'd been bitten. The fever had run its course until the transformation completed. Until he had woken as a vampire, lusting for blood.

He tried to recall what might have happened, whether in all the turmoil of the failed raid he had done something, anything, that could have turned her. Had someone else turned her in his moment of weakness?

Nothing came to mind. Nothing except the fact that there had been blood everywhere, that somehow his blood had contaminated her.

Which left him here, caring for her as her body warred with itself. Fearing that the fevers might still take her. Afraid that if she was at death's door again, he might not be able to let her go.

He'd barely been able to do it the first time.

An hour passed and the spasms seized her once more. As before, he restrained her gently, but she was stronger this time. So strong he had to allow the demon to emerge in order to tame her. The heat of his body bathed hers, which seemed almost cold in comparison to that of the beast. His demon strength subdued her. Held her pinned gently to the bed as she bucked. When she calmed, her eyes opened and she focused on his face. His demon face.

"Ryder. What happened?" Her voice was weak.

He cradled her cheek, her skin still amazingly warm. "I don't know, darlin'."

"Feel...weird," she said. "Cold." As she said that, she yanked at his shirt and begged, "Make me warm. *Por favor.*"

Everything in her system was off kilter, but if his body heat would bring her some relief, he was all for it. He covered her body with his, offering up the demon's heat to soothe her.

She wrapped her arms around him and buried her head against his chest, her teeth chattering. "Cold. Why am I so cold?"

He enveloped her in his arms, brought every inch of their bodies into close contact. Her trembling gradually lessened. She had slipped into a peaceful rest. Beneath his body, the even thrum of her heart beat strongly. Her breath, regular and with more vitality, chilled his demon-heated skin.

He brushed a stray lock of hair from her face and kissed her forehead. Lying beside her, he settled down to rest and await the next round of spasms.

The smell of dawn blowing in on a morning breeze roused him from the bed. An empty bed.

He had been exhausted from a night of keeping Diana in check. It had barely been an hour ago that her temperature had plummeted and calm truly claimed her.

At the foot of the bed were the bandages he had applied the night before.

He rushed in a blast of vamp speed through the doors of his bedroom to the balcony beyond.

Diana stood there, buck-naked. Not a mark of violence marred her body, only the heart-and-knife tattoo on her right shoulder and the pale white line of the long-healed scar along her ribs. She faced the east, waiting for the morning sun.

"What are you doing?"

"What am I, Ryder?" She was too composed for his liking.

He searched for an explanation, but none came.

With a burst of speed almost as fast as his own, she stood in front of him. She cupped his cheek, her palm cold. She ran her thumb along the edge of his fangs. "Am I like this? Did you break your promise?"

"Never." He grasped her arms, but she shrugged out of his embrace and returned to the edge of the balcony, where she once again faced the east.

The first shimmer of sunlight broke over the horizon and the demon within him cowered, urged him to retreat, but he couldn't. Pulling back the beast, he resumed his human form and approached her. Laying a gentle hand on her shoulder, the chill of her skin greeted him. Cooler than human? he wondered, or was his imagination playing games with him?

"Diana?" He needed her to believe that he had kept his word.

I know, came quickly in his mind. "But that still doesn't explain this." She motioned to her unmarred body. "I should be dead."

He couldn't argue with that. "I don't know what happened."

His skin tingled as the sun rose higher and sunlight bathed the balcony. A little brighter and his skin would burn.

"Go, Ryder."

"Diana," he pleaded, wanting her with him, out of the sun's harming rays.

"Go," she repeated, more strongly this time. "I need some time alone."

He was afraid of what would happen to her when the sun fully rose, but she obviously wasn't going to budge.

So you'll just let her fry? his demon voice asked as he walked away. He gritted his teeth and closed his eyes against the vision of a pile of shriveled muscle and bone.

He turned at the French doors and waited, ready to pull her in. But nothing happened as the sun rose. The rays colored the balcony with bright light and she raised her arms to the sky and let the sun's brilliant glow wash over her. Her body fit and whole. Her skin golden with light. With life.

His demon woke as did the human, wanting her like never before.

But as she faced him, he knew she was all business this morning. The warrior had a mission and nothing was going to get in the way.

ADIC Hernandez had called Sebastian to tell him Diana was missing. If he heard from her, he was to tell her to check in. Although it hadn't been said, Diana knew what lay behind those words; She was being sought as a suspect for the botched raid.

How many dead agents? she wondered. She had only vague recollections of what had happened to the two with her and of Alex, wounded and near death inside the apartment.

David? Her gut knotted with guilt. She had failed him much as she had failed Sylvia. Maybe even failed herself, she thought as she looked at her body once more and noted the flawless skin. Flesh unmarred by the violence of the night before.

Ryder had promised and, in her heart, she trusted that he had kept that promise. But her brain… Her brain was telling her everything had gone wrong. With the raid. With Ryder.

She finished dressing in the jeans and shirt Melissa had been kind enough to lend her. They were a size apart, with Melissa being slightly taller and thinner. The pants were long and tight on her curves. The button-down shirt, with its fuller cut, fit just fine. She slipped on her ankle and shoulder holsters. Someone had laundered her FBI windbreaker, but she couldn't run around the city wearing that. Especially if whoever had shot her was on the lookout for her. In Ryder's closet she found a black leather blazer. Big on her, but perfect for hiding the bulge of the gun beneath her arm.

She stepped into the living room where he waited.

"What do you plan to do?"

"There's only one person who could have done this—Hank Rupert."

"How do you know?"

She shrugged. "I just know. Now I have to prove it."

"Do you need me to—"

She held up her hand to silence him. "It's not that I don't appreciate all you've done so far, but this I have to do alone."

Alone. A familiar word with her, Ryder thought. He said nothing else as she walked to the door.

Once there, she paused. "I...I have to go. You understand, right?"

He did. He understood her honor, her determination, the strength of her loyalty to her friends and partner. What he didn't understand was where he would stand after her mission. "Will you be back?"

The answer, when it came, was not unexpected.

"I don't know."

Chapter 25

Diana phoned ADIC Hernandez, certain she could trust him.

"Jesus. Is this line secure?" she asked as soon as he answered.

"Give me a minute."

The muffled sound of his voice instructing someone came across the line. For a second she wondered if he was tracing the call, but she shoved that thought away. She had to trust someone.

"It's not what you think, Jesus. I had nothing to do with what happened."

"Are you okay?"

Was she? she wondered. She was alive, but okay? "I'm fine. What about—"

"Garcia and Harris are in critical condition, but stable. We have five dead agents. The one on the roof with Rupert, the two with you and the two with Harris in the command center."

David and Alex were alive, which brought some small measure of relief. "Rupert?"

"Leg wound. He's still in the hospital, but should be released by tomorrow."

"Don't. Keep him there and make sure the room's wired."

"What? I can't—"

"Trust me. *Por favor.*" She glanced around the surrounding area to make sure no one was headed her way.

"I need proof, Diana."

She thought about what Jesus had just told her. "The slug from Rupert's leg wound?"

"Passed through and into the roof. Too damaged for analysis."

"What about Rupert's gun? Have you fired it for a sample?"

"Do you need me to?"

"Yes. E-mail me a photo of the test bullet and give me a few hours. Don't let Rupert know I'm alive. I want to watch the bastard's face when he sees me." Because she was sure good ol' Hank believed her dead after firing at her.

"Call me when you're ready," he replied, and she hung up.

Plunking a few more coins into the pay phone, she dialed Peter Daly.

Peter handed her the ballistics team's photo of the slug she'd recovered from the floor of the apartment earlier that day. It was the bullet that had passed through her and Ryder and into the padding of the carpet. She laid the photo on the hood of his car directly next to the one Jesus had e-mailed—the slug fired from Rupert's gun.

"Do these look similar to you?"

Peter ran his fingers over the grooves in each. "Same caliber. Same rifling and other distinguishing marks. Same gun fired these."

Together with the file David's contact had e-mailed hours after the raid began, she had more than enough to call Hank's hand. "Thanks for helping me." She grabbed both photos and tucked them into the folder with the e-mail message.

"Do you need anything else?"

She thought about all that had happened in the past dozen or so hours. Thought about what she wanted to do to Hank, and shook her head.

"I think I can handle this, Peter. But thanks again."

He surprised her by embracing her, muttering as he did so, "You don't need to go it alone all the time, Reyes."

Tears came to her eyes. "I know," she said. Surprisingly, she meant it despite the events that had battered not only her body, but her belief system.

When she called her ADIC to find out if Hank's room was ready, he said, "Slipped him something after lunch so he could rest. The room's wired. Agents are ready."

She scanned the late-afternoon traffic snarling the crosstown streets. She'd have to use the subway. "I need about forty-five minutes to get to the hospital."

"I'll be waiting in front."

The file weighed heavily in her hand as she rode the subway downtown, but no more heavily than the uncertainty about what would happen at the hospital or with the rest of her life.

She looked down at her hands again. Her skin remained chilled. But then again, wasn't that a normal human reaction to fear?

Was she afraid? She tightened her hand on the bright steel subway pole until her knuckles were white from the pressure.

Yes, and not just about what would happen in Hank's hospital room. If he didn't break, they would most likely hold her responsible for all that had happened last night. Legally responsible, that was. Whether or not she cleared her name, she would always feel morally responsible. Five innocent men had died because she hadn't identified the threat.

And after? What would there be for her after?

The possible answer to that question scared her even more.

When the train jerked to a halt, she walked the few blocks to the hospital where, as promised, her ADIC waited.

Jesus whispered, "Whatever happens, I will make sure you get justice."

She searched his face for any sign of betrayal. None. She smiled tightly in acknowledgment of his promise and together they entered the hospital. At the door to Hank's room she paused.

"I need to do this alone."

She entered the room and closed the door behind her.

Hank popped up in bed. "Shit, Reyes. I won-dered what had happened to you," he said, a hint of surprise on his face, but not enough. Definitely not enough. He was good, she'd give him that.

"Really?" She ambled to the foot of his bed. "I would think you knew. You tried to kill me."

Hank crossed his arms against his broad chest, but nothing on his face gave away any concern. "You are one *loco* bitch."

"I've been called worse, and by better than you."

She removed the file from under her arm, pulled out the two photos and tossed them in Hank's lap. "Look familiar? Probably not, but let me explain." She motioned to the ballistics photos. "The ones from the three agents you shot were too damaged, as was the one from your leg wound. But the one in the floor of the apartment we raided—the one that missed me—excellent match to your gun."

As she met Hank's gaze, she noticed discom-fort. And disbelief—they both knew his shots had struck home.

"You're lying. Besides, no one will believe you." He negligently tossed the photos back at her.

"How did you shoot yourself, Hank? There

wasn't any evidence of close-range contact, but I know you shot yourself and the other agent. Not to mention the shots you took at me and my team."

"And why would I do that, Special Agent in Charge?"

She tossed another sheath of papers from her file and he caught them against his chest. He blanched. "How did you get this?"

"Only seemed fair that I should know something about you since you seemed to know every-thing about me."

"How did you get this?" he repeated, a little more forcefully.

"A contact e-mailed it to me. Unfortunately, I didn't receive it in time."

"This proves nothing," he replied, and slapped his uninjured leg with the papers.

"Doesn't it? Come on, Hank. Of all people, I know what it's like to want revenge. To want to kill the people responsible for hurting someone you love." She forced a conciliatory tone into her voice.

"Like you want to kill the person who did your friend, Sylvia?" Hank taunted.

A sickening feeling crept into her gut. "You did it, didn't you?"

"Me? Waste my time with such an easy kill? She was out like a light. Not much of a challenge. Shame the baby had to go, as well."

She inched her hand upward, reaching for her gun, wanting uncompromising justice. The dark side of her knew the pain caused by punishment denied. It wouldn't settle for that with Hank. Inside, a foreign heat pooled in her gut as she imagined making him suffer, killing him and avenging Sylvia and her baby. But something stopped her. Something that said she couldn't become a monster like him.

"You want me to kill you, but I won't make it that easy. You deserve to be punished for what you've done."

"What I've done?" he replied calmly. "You don't understand."

"Don't I? I held my father in my arms as he died, Hank. I wanted those people dead. I still do."

"Then why would you want to stop me?" he said, finally showing some sign of agitation. "Why don't you understand why I did this?"

"Your father—"

"Was CIA. Do you know that there are eighty-three stars on the CIA Memorial Wall?" His tone was turbulent. "Eighty-three, but not one of them is for my father."

"He was killed in action?" she asked, although she knew full well what Rupert's father's file said.

"They left him there. Kennedy and his buddies. They sent him there to help the invasion. When it all went to shit, he became expendable."

"You wanted vengeance because the Cubans were responsible for his death."

"Wouldn't you, bitch? You ruined everything," he said, and reached behind him.

She didn't stop to wonder if he had a weapon. He was CIA and probably had an assortment of ways to get what he needed. She should have expected it, but had hoped that he wouldn't…

No, that was a lie. She wanted a reason to kill him.

As Rupert fired, she dodged the bullet with an inhuman burst of speed, but felt its bite along her arm. She drew her own gun, ready for the kill, but found herself shooting to disarm instead. She caught him in the wrist, nearly blowing his hand off. The gun slipped from his grasp, but he reached for it with his other hand.

Jesus Hernandez and another agent barged into the room, weapons drawn. Faced with those odds, Rupert raised his hands in surrender.

It brought little satisfaction and, for a second, she regretted that she hadn't killed him and given him the punishment he deserved.

Jesus helped her upright. She winced as he did so and glanced at her arm. A tear in the leather hinted at the injury below. Lowering the blazer off her shoulder, she noticed the rip in the shirt and the scratch beneath. It was barely bleeding.

"You okay?"

"I'll be fine."

ADIC Hernandez took over, and she walked down the hall to David's room. Through the window, she saw David lying in bed, his girl-friend Maggie beside him.

Diana tapped on the glass and Maggie rushed out of the room and embraced her.

"*Dios,* Di. I thought you were dead."

The wash of Maggie's tears wet the side of Diana's face. "I'm okay."

"Are you? You're cold." Maggie ran her hand along her cheek.

"How's David?" she replied, and stepped back, afraid her observant friend might notice other troubling things besides the cold of her body.

Maggie wiped her tears away. "Critical. Caught a lot of shrapnel from the explosion." Her breath caught in her throat and her next words were strained. "He's paralyzed from the waist down."

"Paralyzed? Is it—"

"Permanent? Probably. We won't know the extent of it until some swelling goes down and they finish up with the medications to try to repair the injury." Maggie reined in a fresh batch of tears with a strangled breath.

"We told him, but he's been so out of it that—"

"You're not sure it really sank in. Can I talk to him?"

Maggie motioned to the door of David's room. "He'll be really glad to see you. He's asked about you a couple of times already."

Her throat choked up with emotion as she approached his bed. His eyes opened and a weak smile came to his face, followed by puzzlement. "Di? You're okay?"

She sat in the chair Maggie had vacated just moments earlier and took David's hand. "I'm fine. You're going to be fine, too."

"Liar," he said, his voice barely above a whisper. "I saw you shot."

"I don't know what happened." She hated lying to him, but then again, she'd been lying to him since the day she had learned Ryder was a vampire. "What happened with you?"

"The room exploded. There was fire everywhere, but I couldn't move. Then two men pulled me out except… Shit, Di. They weren't men."

A chill settled in her gut. "David, you don't know—"

"What they were? You know, don't you?" His voice stronger now, the monitors attached to him beeped furiously with his agitation.

"Please. Calm down." She laid a hand on his chest.

"Tell me. You owe me that much, partner." The way he said the last word sent fear through her.

"I can't. I—"

"Leave." The tone of his voice was frigid, distant.

"Don't do this." Tears came to her eyes at the inflexible set of his jaw.

He met her gaze head-on, his blue eyes blazing with emotion. "I trusted you and look at me." He weakly motioned with his free hand to his mangled body.

"David—" she began, but he cut her off again.

"Until you trust me enough to tell me the truth…just go."

But she couldn't tell him. Instead she dropped a kiss on his cheek. "I do trust you. It's just not my secret to tell. Please understand that."

He turned his face away, providing his answer. Sucking in a rough breath, she walked out, heading across the hall to Alex's room.

There were fewer monitors there, but their steady beep-beep-beep tortured her.

He was awake, and he grinned weakly when he saw her. "I'm glad you're alive."

She brushed a lock of hair from his forehead. "How are you?"

He motioned to the chair beside his bed. "Earned myself a few months R and R, I'm told. I'm also told Lopez is dead and the stolen weapon's been recovered."

"We just nailed Rupert." She explained about the file and why Rupert had been working with the CDA. "I wish we had been able to get that information earlier."

"Heard about your partner. I'm sorry."

She thought about David's parting words. Thought about all that they had shared and how she had failed him. "He's angry. With me."

"Because you didn't tell him about your friend?" Alex asked.

"What friend?" she asked.

Alex laughed, but nothing friendly remained in his tone. "I was pretty out of it myself, but I saw someone. Tall. Dark. Carrying you."

In her scattered memories about the raid, there came a quick flash of seeing Alex, bleeding. Of his eyes, open and staring at her as Ryder carried her past him. "I can't tell you about him."

"Is he the one? Is he the reason—"

"Yes. He's the one."

"Lucky man."

"No questions about who he is or what he was doing there? How it is that I'm here, in one piece?"

"Did David ask all those questions?" Alex scrutinized her as he waited for her answer.

"No. He just asked me to trust him." With those words, what little control she had mustered fled and the tears came. She swiped at them and continued. "If I could tell you—"

"You would? Somehow I don't think so, *amorcito,* but I can deal."

She imagined he could. He'd dealt with her nearly a decade earlier when she'd shut him out. This wasn't much different except that this time, there wouldn't be another chance for them. "I'm glad we got to see each other."

"But you don't want to see me again?"

She weighed her next words carefully before finally saying, "I'm all yours—as a friend. As a colleague."

He smiled sadly. "Until next time, then."

She dropped a quick kiss on his forehead and whispered, "Until next time."

Chapter 26

The sun was long gone by the time she reached Ryder's apartment. She'd been walking for hours, thinking about everything. About David's anger. About Alex's acceptance. About what was in store for her future with her partner injured and her career in shreds. As the Special Agent in Charge, she'd be held accountable for the deaths of the five agents on her team, even though she had solved the case.

She wouldn't quit. Even if they bucked her back to security checks on prospective government employees. She wouldn't quit on David, either. Not when her partner needed her the most.

As she stood in front of Ryder's building, she realized there were just a few more loose ends she had to tie up.

With a wave to the doorman, she went up to Ryder's floor.

He answered, looking tired and anxious. "How are you?"

She shrugged. Yanking at the leather sleeve, she said, "I owe you a blazer."

He eased one hand beneath the jacket to reveal the torn sleeve of Melissa's shirt and the skin beneath, unblemished and totally healed. "You were shot?"

"A scratch only, but here I am," she said with some force as she shoved past him and into his apartment.

"Come on in," he muttered beneath his breath.

She whirled to face him. "I'm sorry. I'm just…David's paralyzed."

He embraced her. "I'm sorry, darlin'. I know how important he is to you."

"He's not talking to me. He knows I was shot. He saw two men—possibly Diego and Blake. He wants to know what they are. How come I'm walking and talking, only…"

"*We* don't know why. Do you want to tell him about me? Explain what I am?"

She did, but not now, when her partner had so much to handle. "Is that okay with you?"

"We need to be okay with it, darlin'."

His words brought comfort and dragged a restrained laugh from her. "Is it a 'we,' Ryder?"

"Do you want it to be?"

She chuckled at the insanity of her situation.
"You made a promise, remember?"

Ryder was at a loss. Maybe it was the lack of
rest or the emotional roller coaster of the night
before that prompted him to say, "I remember
that I want us to live together."

Diana chuckled once again, only this time it
was an exasperated female kind of laugh. She laid
her hands on his shoulders and shook them playfully. "You are such a guy, Ryder. No, not that
promise."

Which brought a smile to his lips as he recollected an earlier promise. The one to which he
hoped she was referring.

"Oh, you mean the one about loving you forever? That promise?"

"Will you? Love me?" she asked, her demeanor suddenly serious.

"I will, and you? Can you commit—"

"To loving you until my last breath? After I was
shot, I knew I was dying. I felt life leaving me
while you held me." Tears came to her eyes and

she finally released her hold on them. "I saw myself in your arms and then…my father was there. Calling me home. I knew that if I went…" She hesitated, a smile on her face despite the tears. "I knew that if I went, I'd be free of the pain of this world. Finally in the light and at peace with myself."

The adoration in her voice twisted something inside of him. Something that wished for all that goodness for her. For himself. Her next words, however, shocked him.

"I didn't ask for the weirdness of this life, Ryder. And I know there's a part of me—and of you—that I will be forever denying. Even with all that…I couldn't go. I couldn't leave you."

"But you would have been free of all this," he said, holding his hands out to everything around them. To all the things that could never bring her the joy that heaven could.

She cradled his face in her hands. "Our journey together isn't over. There's more we have to do."

Impossible to imagine she would sacrifice heaven for him, and yet…she was here. He laid his hands at her waist and drew her into his arms.

"I want to be with you. For as long as that

might be," she said. A shiver worked through her body.

"You okay?"

Her eyes swam with tears waiting to be shed. "How long will that be, now, Ryder? I'm not like you, but I'm not normal anymore, either."

"I don't know, but as long as we're together—"

"We will cherish every morning that we wake in each other's arms." She flashed him that brilliant smile even as the tears spilled down her face. "Together we will handle whatever comes our way."

When Ryder bent his head, she went on tiptoe and met his lips with hers. She pressed herself close, his arms providing her more than she could have imagined. Love. Acceptance. Peace. She knew that when death called again, she would be strong enough to battle it with Ryder and his love beside her.

"Would tomorrow be too soon to move in?" she asked.

Grinning, he whispered against her lips, "Why put off until tomorrow—"

"What you can do today?" She tugged on his

lower lip with her teeth. "It can wait an hour, can't it?"

His mischievous boyish grin said all was right with the world. "Only an hour, love?"

"Okay, maybe later. Much, much later."

After all, they had a lifetime of mornings to share.

* * * * *

Mills & Boon® Intrigue
brings you a sneak preview of…

Caridad Piñeiro's Devotion Calls

Ricardo Fernandez has the power to heal people. But he also has one golden rule – never get entangled in the private lives of people who come to him for help. Despite this, Ricardo can't avoid his attraction to Sara Martinez, a nurse who has brought her terminally ill mother to him for treatment. As the pair embark on a dark adventure, could Sara use her own power to heal Ricardo's heart?

Don't miss this thrilling new story in
THE CALLING *mini-series, available next month in Mills & Boon® Intrigue's new*
NOCTURNE *series.*

Devotion Calls
by
Caridad Piñeiro

Spanish Harlem, New York City

The saints' eyes followed him as he worked, scolding him for using them for his lie. Mocking him for denying the truth about what he was.

Ricardo Fernandez paused and laid his hands on the altar that embodied the fraud that was his life. All around him the statues of the saints condemned him. But he was used to such censure from those who refused to believe in his powers. Those whose fears forced him to hide behind the guise of a *santero*.

He looked down at his hands and, as he had countless times in his thirty years of life, considered why he had been chosen to carry this burden. Why these hands, which looked just like those of any other man, possessed the power to give life or take it away.

If he was a lesser man, he might have fallen into the trap of considering himself almost godlike. He might have opted to sell his abilities to those who paid the highest price to be saved. He could have even made a perfect assassin, able to kill without leaving a trace.

But Ricardo had done none of those things. Neither regrets nor revelry had a place in his life now, so he resumed his task. With a gentle touch, he removed the offerings he had placed on the altar the day before: the fine cigar, now just a half-burned stub and a pile of ashes, and the shot glass of fragrant rum, which had nearly evaporated from the heat of the radiator just a few feet away. After checking the water level in the vase of sunflowers he had placed beside one *virgencita,* he shifted to the last offering.

A small pile of coins lay at the foot of one statue. He gathered up the money in his hand and thanked the deity. While he himself was not a true believer in Santería, his customers held to this faith and he wouldn't besmirch their tenets. He hoped his prayer was deemed respectful enough by the deities that allowed him to use the powers with which he had been born.

Ricardo didn't like living a lie, but posing as a *santero*—a priest of the Afro-Caribbean religious

Santería—was the only way he could use his healing gifts. Many of the people who sought him out might not have come to him if they realized his abilities were earthly. They preferred to think the powers came from rituals beseeching their gods.

Of course, if some god hadn't decided to give him this boon, who had? Ricardo refused to consider the alternative, since he had sworn never to use the dark side of his gift. Not even when someone asked for it.

As had happened just the other day with Evita Martinez.

He had been seeing Evita for just over a year now, ever since the doctors at one of New York City's more prestigious hospitals had told her that there was nothing else they could do for her cancer. They'd sent her home to enjoy what was left of her life.

But Evita hadn't wanted to die just yet. Having heard about his unique abilities from some of the other ladies in the neighborhood, she had come to him for help. She and her daughter, Sara.

Sara, he thought with a sigh, recalling the way she had stood before him nearly a year ago, condemning him with her body language as he talked about what he could and could not do for Evita.

He knew that Sara hadn't believed him. Worse, that she considered him a charlatan. Her bright hazel eyes had skewered him with disbelief, much like those of the saints.

The disbelief in her eyes turned to trepidation when, after finding out that she was a nurse, he had asked for payment of a most unusual kind—blood. For a moment he'd thought she might run, and take her mother with her, but then despair had crept into her eyes.

Sara loved her mother, and at that moment she had been desperate enough to do anything to help her— even if it meant bringing bags of blood to a man she considered less than dirt. Ricardo hated relying on that despair. He hated the lying, but he did what he had to so he could help people.

When Sara brought a blood bag later today, he would have to tell the prickly nurse that her mother's cancer was growing faster than he could contain it, and that Evita had asked him to help her pass peacefully when the time came, rather than suffer with the pain.

Healing and killing. His gift and his curse.

A tap sounded against the glass of his door. He turned from the altar and stared toward the front of his store.

Sara Martinez stood there, her chin tucked into the thick collar of the charcoal-gray down jacket she wore against the lingering chill of winter. A crazy gust of March wind sent her silky shoulder-length brown hair swirling around her face. With a gloved hand, she combed it back and shifted from foot to foot, impatient and intractable as always about these visits.

The early morning sun played across her pretty,

heart-shaped face. She had a hint of a cleft in her chin, and hazel eyes that expressed so much with just a look. In his case, generally disgust. But he had seen how those eyes could warm to a molten caramel when they gazed upon someone she loved.

And her lips… They were full, at least most of the time. Not when she shot him a grim look, as she did right now as she waited at his door.

Drawing a deep breath, he prepared himself to break the news that would surely devastate her.

1	2	3	4	5	6	7	8	9	10	11	12
13	14	15	16	17	18	19	20	21	22	23	24
25	26	27	28	29	30	31	32	33	34	35	36
37	38	39	40	41	42	43	44	45	46	47	48
49	50	51	52	53	54	55	56	57	58	59	60
61	62	63	64	65	66	67	68	69	70	71	72
73	74	75	76	77	78	79	80	81	82	83	84
85	86	87	88	89	90	91	92	93	94	95	96
97	98	99	100	101	102	103	104	105	106	107	108
109	110	111	112	113	114	115	116	117	118	119	120
121	122	123	124	125	126	127	128	129	130	131	132
133	134	135	136	137	138	139	140	141	142	143	144
145	146	147	148	149	150	151	152	153	154	155	156
157	158	159	160	161	162	163	164	165	166	167	168
169	170	171	172	173	174	175	176	177	178	179	180
181	182	183	184	185	186	187	188	189	190	191	192
193	194	195	196	197	198	199	200	201	202	203	204
205	206	207	208	209	210	211	212	213	214	215	216
217	218	219	220	221	222	223	224	225	226	227	228
229	230	231	232	233	234	235	236	237	238	239	240
241	242	243	244	245	246	247	248	249	250	251	252
253	254	255	256	257	258	259	260	261	262	263	264
265	266	267	268	269	270	271	272	273	274	275	276
277	278	279	280	281	282	283	284	285	286	287	288
289	290	291	292	293	294	295	296	297	298	299	300
301	302	303	304	305	306	307	308	309	310	311	312
313	314	315	316	317	318	319	320	321	322	323	324
325	326	327	328	329	330	331	332	333	334	335	336
337	338	339	340	341	342	343	344	345	346	347	348
349	350	351	352	353	354	355	356	357	358	359	360
361	362	363	364	365	366	367	368	369	370	371	372
373	374	375	376	377	378	379	380	381	382	383	384
385	386	387	388	389	390	391	392	393	394	395	396
397	398	399	400	401	402	403	404	405	406	407	408
409	410	411	412	413	414	415	416	417	418	419	420

FREE

4 BOOKS AND A SURPRISE GIFT!

We would like to take this opportunity to thank you f...
Mills & Boon® book by offering you the chance to take...
specially selected titles from the Intrigue series abs...
We're also making this offer to introduce you to the b...
Mills & Boon® Book Club—

- ★ **FREE home delivery**
- ★ **FREE gifts and competitions**
- ★ **FREE monthly Newsletter**
- ★ **Books available before they're in the shops**
- ★ **Exclusive Mills & Boon® Book Club offers**

Accepting these FREE books and gift places you under no obligation to buy; you may cancel at any time, even after receiving your free shipment. Simply complete your details below and return the entire page to the address below. You don't even need a stamp!

YES! Please send me 4 free Intrigue books and a surprise gift. I understand that unless you hear from me, I will receive 6 superb new titles every month for just £3.15 each, postage and packing free. I am under no obligation to purchase any books and may cancel my subscription at any time. The free books and gift will be mine to keep in any case.

I8ZEE

Ms/Mrs/Miss/Mr..........................Initials ....

BLOCK CAPITALS PLEASE

Surname ....

Address ....

....

....Postcode ....

Send this whole page to:
The Mills & Boon Book Club, FREEPOST CN81, Croydon, CR9 3WZ